DALYA
and the
the Magic
INK
BOTTLE

J.M. EVENSON

Raintree is an imprint of Capstone Global Library Limited, a company incorporated in England and Wales having its registered office at 264 Banbury Road, Oxford, OX2 7DY – Registered company number: 6695582

www.raintree.co.uk
myorders@raintree.co.uk

Designed by Tracy McCabe
Original illustrations © Capstone Global Library Limited 2021
Originated by Capstone Global Library Ltd
Printed and bound in India

978 1 3982 0198 9

British Library Cataloguing in Publication Data
A full catalogue record for this book is available from the British Library.

Acknowledgements
Cover illustration by Craig Phillips.

For L.M.E. and L.M.E.

1

TWO EYES IN THE DARK

The mansion looked like it was straight out of a spooky horror film.

It stood in the middle of an overgrown courtyard crowded with dead weeds, hidden from view as though it had been lost in a time warp. Paint peeled from the grey exterior in curly ribbons. The roof buckled on one side. Black plastic gaped over the downstairs window. The front door slanted like a crooked tooth.

The mansion had slithering mist, tangled trees and creepy shadows – all that was missing was thunder and some scary music. It was heinous, dreadful, sinister, ghastly. There weren't enough words to describe how awful it was. In the dictionary under *spooky*, there was probably a picture of this house.

And I was supposed to live here *all summer*.

I nervously clutched the handle of my purple suitcase. This place was bad news. I could feel it in my bones. One thing was for sure: This was not going to be a good holiday.

"What do you think?" my dad asked with a hesitant smile.

He was tall with wavy brown hair and hazel eyes that turned up at the sides like a cat's. When I was little, people used to tell me that we looked alike, but I didn't see it.

I scowled at him. "You're joking, right?"

This trip had been my dad's idea. I hadn't wanted to go, but he'd insisted on taking me to his family's ancestral home in Istanbul, Turkey. The city sat on the border between Europe and Asia, which he'd pointed out when he showed me where it was on a map. Somehow, though, he'd forgotten to mention we'd be staying in a seriously creepy house. That seemed like information he might've shared in advance, but I guess he didn't think about how I'd react.

I couldn't believe he'd spent his childhood in this house and never talked about it. Then again, he had never said much about his Turkish family. He was almost always too distracted with work to answer questions about why he'd left Istanbul.

Pretty much all I knew about my dad was that he'd come to the United States when he was twenty-two years old to get his medical degree, and now he was a doctor who did cancer research at a clinic in Cleveland. When I was five years old, he'd become the director of his department, and a year later my mum divorced him. Between the divorce and his hospital schedule, he'd barely told me anything. All I knew was that his parents had passed away when he was young, and he was an only child like me. The scary mansion explained a few things, though. I could see why he'd wanted to get away from a place like this.

Not knowing much about my dad usually didn't bother me because I lived with my mum, and we were happy, except for the part where she wouldn't let me get a dog because she was allergic. My mum was a lawyer and worked a lot too, but she always came home on time and didn't mind if I ate dinner in my room as long as I was reading.

Summer holidays were supposed to be spent with my dad, but this was the first time he'd taken me up on it. Usually I spent summers at home doing whatever I wanted. I'd thought my mum would definitely protest when my dad proposed taking me halfway around the globe, but instead she'd made plans for a cruise in the Caribbean with her new boyfriend. It would've been nice if someone had asked me what I wanted. I would've picked the cruise over the freaky mansion, thank you very much, but I didn't have a choice.

If my dad had at least taken me to a decent hotel, things might've been okay. We could've visited the tourist attractions and gone home, no problem. But no. This trip was the one time he'd felt like paying attention to me, and he'd brought me here, to this spooky house.

A damp breeze kicked up and goosebumps prickled down my neck. A tickle twisted in my gut, like someone was looking over my shoulder. I glanced around the courtyard, searching for anything moving, but there was nothing there. Shivers raced up my spine as I tugged at the rumpled hem of my shirt. I was embarrassingly tall for a twelve-year-old, so shirts rarely fitted me properly.

There had to be a way to convince my dad to get back on the plane and go home. I set my chin and steadied my voice, then turned to him. "Baba, I think we should leave."

Baba was the Turkish word for *father*. It was one of the few words I knew in his language, and I'd called him that for as long as I could remember.

"Leave? Why?" Baba's eyes crinkled with surprise.

I took a deep breath. Time for the truth. "It looks haunted," I said matter-of-factly.

"You've been reading too many books about castles and witches. The house isn't haunted. It's just old." Baba chuckled. "Let's go inside and meet your great aunt Zehra."

Going inside was the last thing I wanted to do. "We could go to a hotel."

"I already told Aunt Zehra we'd be staying here."

I wasn't sure I wanted to meet anyone who would live in a place like this, even if they were supposed to be family. "So?" I said.

"So, she's excited to meet you."

"Couldn't we come back tomorrow, during the day? When the sun is up?" Sunlight wouldn't fix everything, but at least it wouldn't be dark.

"I told you, Dalya, we need to stay here because my aunt needs help selling the house."

"Why can't she do it herself?"

Baba was getting irritated. I could see it in his face. "She just can't. You'll see why." He grunted as he shifted a heavy duffle bag from one arm to the other. "Everywhere around here is closed. It's the middle of the night. Let's go inside. I'm tired and it's getting cold."

"But – "

As I opened my mouth to object, a twig snapped behind me. I jerked my head to look.

"Did you hear that?" I whispered.

"Hear what?" He looked at me quizzically.

I held still, straining my ears, while my heart did a drumroll along my ribs. Even the silence around here was eerie. It was too quiet, like being underwater. "We could go back to the airport and stay there."

"You're being ridiculous, Dalya." Baba tottered towards the house, weighed down with luggage.

He was going to leave me there in the courtyard. I couldn't believe it.

I hesitated, watching him make his way up the stairs. I didn't want to go inside, but I didn't want to be left alone outside either. I had to make a decision fast.

Silhouetted trees rattled with a gust of wind, their branches bowing and swaying like dancing skeletons as a silver crescent moon peeked out from behind a cloud. I was still queasy from the long flight from Ohio.

I didn't want to admit it, but Baba was right: I had been reading a lot of horror stories lately. Maybe I was letting my imagination run away with me. There was no reason to be scared – it was just an old house.

Just an old house. I let those words hang in my mind for a moment, but I didn't quite believe them.

To be safe, I thought it was better to stay with Baba. I tipped my suitcase forwards on its wheels and sprinted after him.

"Hello?" Baba pushed open the front door. His voice rang out in a large, empty entrance hall that was dimly lit by a rusty chandelier missing all but two of its three dozen light bulbs. The curtains hung in shreds. A grey rug spread under our feet. I couldn't even guess what colour it had originally been. Across the hall was the widest and tallest staircase I'd ever seen. The banister curled at the bottom like a dragon's tail.

The woodwork was amazing – swirls and whirls of fancy carved patterns. I couldn't have explained it, but the place felt familiar, as if I'd seen it somewhere before, maybe in a dream. Someone had built this beautiful place, and someone had let it go to ruin. Why?

Everything about the house was a mystery, just like my dad. Two complete unknowns. Some part of me didn't care to know. And yet … a flicker of curiosity sparked in my chest.

I craned my neck, trying to get a look upstairs. The first floor vanished into blackness.

"What's up there?" I asked.

"Nothing." I turned towards the dark hallway as an elderly woman squeaked forwards in a wheelchair. She had thick glasses that made her eyes seem huge and red lipstick that was slightly crooked, but she held her shoulders stiff and properly, like a lady.

A wide smile spread on her face.

"Murat!" she exclaimed. "It's good to see you. Thank you for coming."

"Of course I came." Baba bent down to hug her, and they chattered away in Turkish as he wrapped an arm around me. He beamed like he was showing off a prize at the fair.

I waited next to him awkwardly. I didn't speak any Turkish apart from calling him "Baba". He'd tried to teach me a few words here or there when I was younger, but then he'd got busy at work and he hadn't had time to give me lessons. A couple of years had gone by and I'd forgotten almost every word he'd ever taught me. I was going to spend our whole holiday completely clueless.

Baba watched me for a moment like he could guess what I was thinking, then he switched back to English. "I should've brought Dalya here sooner to meet you, Zehra Hala."

She stretched out a frail hand to me. It suddenly made sense why she needed help selling her house. Looking at her, I understood.

"Dalya is here now. That's all that matters. Now, let's see our girl." She patted my hand gently. Her accent was heavy, but her voice was slow and sure. "I am your Great Aunt Zehra. In Turkish, you should call me Zehra Hala. Come. You must be hungry, my child."

"I'm not." That wasn't true. My stomach gurgled, but I wanted to get a look at my room and do a thorough check under the bed for spiders before I turned out the lights. An old place like this almost certainly had a lot of spiders. Better to be safe than sorry.

"You sure you don't want anything?" Baba asked.

"I'm sure."

"Okay. I'll bring in the rest of our luggage." He went back outside to get the suitcase he'd left at the front.

Zehra Hala swivelled towards the hallway, then stopped and fished around in her pocket. "I've forgotten the extra key for your father. I have so few guests anymore – I don't even know how to behave when they turn up. I'll be right back."

She wheeled out of the room, leaving me alone in the entrance hall. I gazed uneasily at the dusty staircase, rolling my suitcase back and forth anxiously, waiting for her to return. She was taking a long time.

There was probably not *nothing* upstairs. If the mansion was as ancient as it looked, then someone was bound to have left something behind. Hopefully it wasn't an angry spirit. In horror stories, forbidden areas in mansions were always filled with evil spirits.

The spark of curiosity – I felt it again when I glanced up there. I squinted, trying to adjust to the low light, as I cautiously placed a foot on the first step and leaned forwards to get a better look. The wood let out a squeal. I snatched my foot back and whirled around to find Zehra Hala glaring at me. She blinked her enormous magnified eyes.

"The floors upstairs are rotted," she said sternly. "The last person who went up there took a wrong step and fell straight through the floor to the kitchen below. He landed on top of the cooker in a pot of steaming stew."

I gawked at her in surprise, unable to tell if she was joking or not. "That sounds painful."

"He was fine, just a few broken bones and a burn." Zehra Hala leaned close. "Go upstairs at your own risk, Dalya. There are more dangerous things in this world than rotted floors."

Like what? It sounded like she had something specific in mind. Giving the staircase one last glance, I turned to follow her down several long hallways to a bedroom. As she unlocked the door, the hinges screeched.

"Good night, my dear." Before I could say anything, Zehra Hala disappeared, leaving me alone again. I hovered in the hallway, not knowing what to do. For a moment I considered going back to the entrance hall to see if I could find Baba, but he'd probably say I was being ridiculous – again. Still, I hoped my dad would be back soon.

My legs were so tired they were nearly shaking, so I turned to check out my room. It wasn't much larger than a walk-in wardrobe, but it was clean. A red tulip painting hung on the wall and a frilly yellow blanket decorated the twin bed nestled by the window. I'd always loved yellow. For some reason it made me feel warm, like sunshine. Everything considered, my room could've been a lot worse. I sank down on the bed and put on my pyjamas, then sifted through my luggage until I found my book and the peanut butter sandwich I'd packed. Peanut butter was my favourite.

Cracking the book open, I slumped on the bed and thumbed

through the pages while I munched on my snack and tried to pretend that I wasn't listening to every creak in the house.

Baba opened my door and poked his head in. "Everything okay?"

I debated telling him the truth. "You told me before we came here that we would only stay until you sold the place. How long is that going to be?"

"I don't know."

"You really think you're going to find a buyer?" I wrinkled my nose at him sceptically.

"The house isn't the reason they'll buy it," he explained. "We've got an acre of prime land in the middle of the city. Trust me, there will be buyers."

"Okay, but how long will it take?"

An uneasy frown passed across Baba's face. He spoke as though he'd rehearsed the words. "We haven't had much time together in a while – "

That was an understatement.

"But," he continued, "I was hoping we could use this trip to reconnect."

I stifled a groan. "Reconnecting" sounded like it would involve a lot of awkward conversations about feelings.

"I know I've been spending a lot of time working, but I thought this trip might help me change. Does that make sense?" he asked. He seemed to be pleading.

I stared at him. I'd seen that frown before. The week before my parents told me about the divorce, Baba had spent a weekend looking at new flats. When I'd asked him what was going on, he'd got the same look on his face.

Nothing about this trip made sense to me. But it didn't matter – the most important thing was for him to concentrate on selling the house so we could go back home. I crossed my arms and swallowed my feelings. "Okay," I said flatly.

He broke into a relieved smile before he paused again. "I should warn you: Zehra Hala is a little bit . . . unusual."

"Yeah. I got that."

"When I was a boy, she always used to talk about some big family secret."

That didn't sound good. I bunched my eyebrows together. "I'm listening."

"There's nothing to worry about. She's a nutty old lady who tells nutty old stories." He ruffled my hair. "Take whatever she says with a grain of salt, but make sure you try her Turkish apple tea. She makes the best tea."

In my experience, whenever someone told me not to worry, it meant I should start worrying immediately.

"Try to get some rest." He switched off the light and closed the door behind him.

I shook off my thoughts, then wormed my way between the cold sheets. I was exhausted. My head felt like it was stuffed with cotton wool. I looked at the ceiling, waiting for sleep. Barely visible in the far corner was a faint trace of a water stain shaped like an animal with two pointed ears. The blanket smelled musty. I wondered if we could get it washed tomorrow.

I shifted towards the wall and punched the pillow, trying to get comfortable.

Then, as my body stilled and I was about to drift off, a loud knock rattled the window. I bolted upright, my muscles tense.

I put on my slippers and darted across the room to flick on the light, removing the lampshade for maximum brightness. Then I stepped forwards, forcing myself to look outside.

Out in the dark, two eyes glowed like fire. One eye was brilliant blue, like a summer sky. The other was yellow, like glittering gold. No body, no face – just two burning eyes.

"Oh!" I stumbled backwards, stunned, as a shape came into focus. It had snow white fur, triangle ears, a pink mouth, glossy whiskers and a black-tipped tail that twitched every once in a while as if it were alive.

A cat, nothing more.

I breathed deeply, relieved.

The animal watched me with its odd-coloured eyes, blinking slowly, as if it were trying to make a decision. I opened the window and held out my hand, then waited. If I was quiet enough, it might come inside and let me pet it. I could definitely use a friend.

The cat was thin and scrawny, its ribs showing and its sides hollow as spoons. It had to be hungry, so I crumbled the crust of my sandwich and sprinkled it on the windowsill. The cat sniffed the food, then crouched down and gobbled it up. After it was done, it happily licked its lips before it hopped over next to me on the bed and rubbed against my shoulder, purring so loud its whiskers vibrated.

I scratched under its chin.

"You were starving, weren't you?" I had no idea why I was talking to a cat. It seemed silly, but I didn't care.

The cat continued to purr.

I glanced around my tiny room, letting out a sound like a balloon losing its air. "It looks like I'm stuck here."

The cat miaowed.

I kept talking. "You know what I wish? I wish I could go home."

The cat stopped purring. It looked up at me, and I could've sworn I saw it smile.

I tipped my head, confused. "What is it?"

The cat leapt onto the windowsill. Slowly, deliberately, it swished its tail. The black tip began to shine as if it had been dipped in twinkling stars. The cat swished its tail again, releasing a wisp of sparkles that swirled and whirled in twirling curls, making little popping noises, like some kind of fizzy fairy dust.

I gasped.

Opening my hand, I tried to catch some of the dust so I could have a better look. Most of it slipped away, but I caught a few specks. They gleamed like a handful of honey-coloured diamonds.

My hand began to tingle. Then, with a bright flash, the golden dust disappeared.

The tip of the cat's tail stopped shimmering and went back to normal black. I stood still, waiting for its tail to shimmer again, but it didn't.

The cat locked its gaze on me, watching me.

Was I going crazy? I had to be. Maybe my jet lag was worse than I'd thought. Maybe the cat had got into some glitter glue. But didn't glitter get everywhere? There was none on my hands. I was sure I'd seen sparkles dancing in the air – like, well, like *magic*. I turned the thoughts over in my head, wondering if what I'd just seen was real.

As I reached out to touch the cat's tail, it dodged my hand, jumping out of the window and scampering away. I leaned out after it.

"Wait," I said. "Come back!"

The cat gave me one last look, and for a split second, I thought I saw it smile again.

Then it vanished.

2
THE GOOD LUCK CHARM

Something was watching me again. I was sure of it.

My eyes popped open. I snapped upright to look, breathing fast, until I realized the room was empty and quiet. I let out a sigh of relief.

Sunlight edged through the window. I squinted, trying to remember where I was. My eyes focused on the tulip painting and the frilly yellow blanket. *Oh, right,* I thought. *I'm staying in a super creepy house for the summer.*

I'd fallen asleep waiting for the cat to come back. I unwound my legs from the blanket and stuffed my arms into a cardigan, then got up to check Baba's room. He wasn't in it, so I made my way towards the kitchen.

"Baba?" My voice echoed in the silence. "Hello?"

On the counter was a yellow sticky note: *Had to do some errands. Back in a few minutes. Love, Baba.* He'd left me alone? Fantastic. He was back to ignoring me, like he always did when I visited him. So much for reconnecting. I crumpled the note and glanced around.

The kitchen was narrow with floor-to-ceiling windows at either end. Years of use had polished the slick stone floors. A square wooden board was nailed haphazardly to the ceiling above the cooker. That had to be the patched hole Zehra Hala had mentioned – the one the man had fallen through when he'd been walking around upstairs. I grabbed an apple from the worktop and wandered towards the entrance hall.

My neck hairs bristled. There it was again – the feeling of being watched. Something scratched behind me. My heart skittered in my chest as I turned towards the sound.

It was coming from behind a pair of sliding wooden doors. Cautiously, I nosed inside. It was an old ballroom. Blue-and-white ceramic tiles lined the walls. Green glass tiles decorated the ceiling. Red marble lined the floors. Lavender perfume clung to the dust.

Scratch, scratch.

I whipped around. Now the noise was coming from the front door. Something was trying to get inside. A small animal, maybe . . . a *cat?*

As I opened the door to look, a flash of white fur flitted down the steps and disappeared behind a tree. It *was* the cat.

Scrambling out through the door, I raced towards the tree and peeked behind it, but the cat wasn't there. I scanned the outside area, trying to guess where it might've gone.

The courtyard was mostly empty. Everything in sight was leafless and bare except for a lemon tree next to the porch. Its branches sagged with brown-spotted lemons.

A crumbling brick wall ringed the courtyard. It had a rusty iron door and an O-ring knocker, like an ancient castle gate.

I turned my gaze back to the run-down mansion. The cat could be hiding under the front porch, or maybe in one of the dead bushes. Making my way carefully through the brambles, I searched the leafy tangles until I came full circle, back to the gate. The cat was nowhere to be found.

Leaning down, I took a closer look at the gate. At the bottom, there was a square cut out of the wood, like a cat-sized door. This had to be how it got in and out, since the wall was too high to jump over. If the cat wasn't inside the courtyard, maybe it was outside. I opened the gate to look.

A wave of sight, sound and smell rushed at me. People hurried this way and that on the cobblestone street. I couldn't believe how fast they were walking – nobody I knew walked that fast in Ohio – and most of them were carrying armfuls of grocery bags stuffed with fruit and vegetables.

Eight cars packed the narrow street, all of them honking. To my left was a traffic light, but the junction was laid out like a wheel, with streets shooting out in all directions. I couldn't imagine how anyone remembered which way was north or south.

Frying oil smoked up the air. Across from me, a man stood behind a cart, layering his sizzling grill with silver-skinned fish. Above him, a woman wearing an orange scarf leaned over her balcony and shouted something in Turkish at him as she gathered towels from the drying rack. He waved back, smiling, and they began chatting loudly.

It had never occurred to me that my hometown was quiet and small, but compared to this city, it definitely was. Here, there was so much happening all at once, so many new sights and sounds, it felt like my brain was overloading. I blinked, all my thoughts mashing together in a noisy haze.

I grabbed the O-ring handle and swung the gate shut with a bang.

Not only was I stuck in a spooky house, I was also trapped in a noisy, big city. This holiday was getting worse by the minute. Also, I hadn't found the cat.

"Dalya!" Zehra Hala called from the front door and waved for me to come inside. "I have prepared a proper breakfast for you. Come. Sit down and eat, and I will tell you our family secret."

Food sounded good. A "family secret" sounded even better. Baba had warned me Zehra Hala liked to tell nutty tales, but I couldn't resist.

I jogged after her as she rolled down the hallway in her wheelchair, the wood floors creaking under the weight. We rounded the corner to the kitchen, where the table was set. I sank into a chair as she hummed something that sounded like "Somewhere Over the Rainbow".

She winked at me. "You recognize the tune, don't you? That is what you're thinking."

Actually, I'd been thinking she'd promised to tell me the family secret and I was waiting for it. I was even pretending to be patient.

She hummed some more. "It is a song from *The Wizard of Oz*. I must have watched it a hundred times. That is how I learned to speak English – by watching American films."

That didn't seem possible. Then again, I didn't know any foreign languages, so maybe it was. I supposed it might be possible to learn Turkish this way, if Baba allowed me enough screen time, but he wouldn't. He'd given me a speech on the plane about television being terrible for my brain.

Even if I did learn Turkish, I'd never feel comfortable on those busy streets outside the courtyard.

Zehra Hala set a bread basket in front of me. "Have you seen *The Wizard of Oz*?"

I nodded.

"It's one of my favourites," she continued. "However, there was always something that bothered me at the end. Dorothy clicks her heels and says, 'There's no place like home', but this is wrong."

Wrong? I pinched my eyebrows together. There was no way that was wrong. It was the rightest thing in the whole film – I knew it because I felt it. If I could've clicked my heels three times and been back in Ohio, where everything was calm and familiar, I would've.

"You don't believe me." She gave me a thoughtful look. "I will tell you what I think. Any place can be home if you keep an open heart. Home is wherever you find love and friendship."

I was quiet. This didn't seem true to me, but I couldn't see the point in saying so. The important thing was to survive the summer. Istanbul didn't need to feel like home.

She smiled warmly at me. "You will get used to this place, little by little, my dear. I promise." She picked up a pair of silver tongs and gestured to the spread. "Now, we shall eat. You haven't lived until you've tasted freshly baked Turkish bread."

"Thank you." I took a slice of bread and bit into it. The crust was buttery and crunchy, and the centre was soft as a cloud. She was right – it was delicious.

She leaned forwards. "Now, I will tell you the family secret."

Finally. "Yes, please," I said.

"First, I would like to give you something," she said.

I shifted in my chair impatiently. I didn't want gifts; I wanted the secret.

Zehra Hala pulled a worn velvet box from her pocket and handed it to me. Inside was a necklace with a circular glass pendant that had three rings of colour. The outer ring was blue, the smaller one was white, and the centre was black. The glass gave it a watery look, like it was filled with tears. I rolled the pendant back and forth between my fingers. It reminded me of a blue eye, and it appeared to be tracking me. I knew it was an illusion, but it was fascinating. Maybe a little unsettling too.

"Do you know what this is?" she asked. "It's a good luck charm. Let me see you put it on."

I took the necklace out of the box and fastened it around my neck.

She beamed at me. "You look very much like your Baba.

You have the same hazel eyes. My mother, your great-great grandmother, had the same eyes too. There's a painting of her in the hallway."

I couldn't help frowning. I'd always hated it when people said I looked like Baba. We might have the same eye colour, but that's where it ended. As far as I could tell, we were nothing alike.

"It's true, my dear. You belong in this family." She touched my cheek. "You are beautiful, my child. Mashallah."

She said the word in a hushed voice, repeating it over and over again, *mashallah, mashallah*, soft and reverent, as if the word were so powerful it had to be whispered. But I had no idea what it meant.

"I am giving you this necklace because *you* are the key to the family secret," she said.

My mouth twisted in confusion. *"Me?"*

She leaned closer. "Something here is watching you. You can feel it, can't you?"

I had felt it. But how did she know? A shudder sped down my spine as my voice shrank to a whisper. "What's watching me?" I asked.

Zehra Hala clamped onto my arm. "You will set things right for our family. I have seen it in a dream. It will be a dangerous adventure, but you must do it."

"What do you mean, 'set things right'? What kind of 'adventure'?" I demanded.

"This, you must discover for yourself."

"Tell me now." My voice accidentally came out like a childish whine. My cheeks scorched with embarrassment. "It doesn't make sense – "

"Ah! Here is your Baba," said Zehra Hala.

Baba stood in the doorway. "You aren't filling her head with nonsense, are you, Zehra Hala?"

I scowled at him. He'd returned at the exact wrong time. She was just about to tell me the most important part – and he'd interrupted her.

"There is only one kind of nonsense in this world, and it is people who don't believe in kismet." She winked sideways at me, then smiled sweetly at him. "Excuse me, Dalya, but I should rest. We will continue this conversation later."

"Wait. What's kismet? You can't leave – " I protested.

"I promise to tell you more, after my rest." She wheeled out through the doorway.

I made an angry face at Baba. "Zehra Hala was in the middle of telling me something."

Baba sat down and loaded his plate with olives and cheese. "Was it one of her wacky family stories? I told you – "

"It wasn't wacky," I replied testily. "What's kismet?"

He spoke around a mouthful of feta cheese. "Doesn't mean anything."

If Zehra Hala said it, then it must mean *something*. I crossed my arms and drummed my fingers at him expectantly.

His face softened after he swallowed. "It means *fate*. Zehra Hala believes we all have some mysterious destiny to fulfil."

He hesitated. "Listen, Dalya, I have some bad news. There's something I have to do for work."

I jerked my eyes to his. "What?"

"It's just for today," he said.

"But you said you wanted to change things. To *reconnect* or whatever."

"Things will change slowly. You have to be patient."

I glared at him. I'd been patient for six years. "But . . ." I struggled for words. There had to be somewhere he wanted to go with me – I didn't care where. "You told me you wanted to show me around the neighbourhood where you grew up."

"I know you're disappointed – "

"You don't know anything about me!"

A cloud passed over Baba's face, as though he was worried that I might be right. His phone buzzed in his pocket. He sat still, watching me, his mouth frozen as if he wanted to say something, but then his phone buzzed again.

"I'm sorry, love. I'll finish up here, and we'll go somewhere tonight," he said.

Sure. Unless something else came up. "What am I supposed to do today?"

"Entertain yourself," he said. His phone buzzed insistently. "Remember to stay downstairs. The floors upstairs aren't safe."

He pushed the answer button on his phone and walked down the hall. "Hi, David. I'm glad you caught me . . ." His voice trailed off as he disappeared.

I scowled. That was great, just great. Not even twenty-four

hours into the holiday, and he'd already started working again.

I was still hungry, so I filled a napkin with a few extra slices of bread and made my way to my bedroom. Halfway down the hall, I dropped a slice. Standing back up after I'd grabbed it, I noticed an oval-shaped portrait of a girl on the top shelf of a bookcase. The girl had wavy brown hair and hazel eyes, and she was wearing a pink satin dress embroidered with silver thread. Zehra Hala had said there was a painting of my great-great grandmother in the hallway, so this had to be it.

I was about to turn away when I noticed something in the girl's lap.

It was a cat with white fur, triangle ears, pink nose, glossy whiskers, and a black-tipped tail. One of its eyes was brilliant blue and the other was glittering gold. The painting looked about a hundred years old, but the cat in her lap was nearly identical to the one I had seen last night. I stared at it, surprised. Maybe I was wrong. I needed to get a closer look.

As I stepped on a lower shelf and pulled myself up, a decorative silver tray crashed to the floor. I snatched it up to inspect it for damage, then paused to look at my reflection, moving the silver tray from side to side as my face stretched and scrunched like a fun house mirror, wondering if I could see what Zehra Hala had seen in me.

She'd tried to convince me I looked like Baba, but she was wrong – I wasn't like him. The necklace she'd given me was pretty, but it didn't mean I belonged in the family. There was no way I was the "family secret". And yet . . . she was right about one thing. I *had* felt something watching me. What was it, and what did it want? I wrapped my cardigan tightly around me, trying to ward off a shiver.

Scratch, scratch. Claws on wood again.

Goosebumps snaked down my arm as I turned around. The sound was coming from above. I tipped my head.

At the top of the stairs, two glowing eyes floated in the air, one blue and the other gold. A shadow split from the dark and slid into silhouetted form. *The cat.* I smiled as it took a seat on the top step and peered down at me.

"There you are," I whispered.

Holding my gaze, the cat swished its tail, scattering a fizzy puff of sparkling gold dust that danced in the air.

I froze. It was the same thing I'd seen the night before – but now I knew I hadn't imagined it, because I'd seen it twice.

Baba had told me not to go up there. Zehra Hala had warned me it wasn't safe. There were a thousand reasons to stay downstairs.

The cat twitched its tail, the tip curling like a beckoning finger. It sat as still as a statue at the top of the stairs. Only the light in its eyes moved, flickering with a peculiar intensity.

My heart fluttered against my ribcage like a bird trying to escape, but there was really no question about what I was going to do.

3
STRANGE AND TRUE

The staircase definitely did not look safe, so I needed a strategy. Some of the steps were partly rotted and others had nails jutting out at odd angles. If I hopscotched around the bad areas, though, I could make it. As I stepped on the first stair, the wood let out a groan. I waited, listening to see if anyone was coming, but the house was silent. I put my other foot on the next stair, and then the next, testing each one before putting my weight on it. Slowly and carefully, I made my way up. Just before I got to the top, the cat whirled around and darted down the hallway on the left.

"Come back!" I whispered, but it was already gone.

I studied the floors, remembering the story Zehra Hala had told me about someone falling through. Blackened lines streaked the wood, as if mould had grown between the boards, and in a few places the wood looked like it had been eaten by termites. Most of the rot was concentrated in the middle, though, so if I skirted along the sides, I could avoid it.

Across from me was a dusty stained-glass window covered

with cobwebs that fluttered like gloomy veils. On the floor below was a patched-up hole that matched the one I'd seen in the kitchen. I could step over it, but there might be other unsafe spots I didn't know about. Zehra Hala had told me the whole first floor was dangerous, and it wasn't as if I'd checked the ceilings in all the rooms downstairs.

Spreading my arms along the wall, I took a cautious step to the left. Specks of dust wheeled in swirling eddies as I slid sideways. I glanced around the corner to see if I could spot the cat, but it had disappeared into one of the rooms. The only question was which one. I kneeled next to a set of fresh pawprints in the dust. They led down the hallway, past two open doors, and abruptly stopped at the third, which was shut.

That was odd. I was pretty sure cats didn't know how to open and shut doors.

Shuffling along the wall, I positioned myself across from the door. The rot looked pretty bad right there, so it didn't seem like a good idea to try stepping on it. In order to reach it, I'd have to jump. Crouching down, I gathered my strength, then leapt forwards and landed – as a snapping sound broke the silence. Under my feet, a split in the floorboard widened. I grabbed the doorknob and shoved it open, scrambling into the room, only to screech to a halt as I nearly tripped over a jagged hole the size of a boot. I held on to the door, teetering dangerously close to it and smothering a yelp. Below, through the hole, I could see Baba's bedroom.

He was sitting directly underneath me. The floorboards let

out another squeak. He had to have heard the creaks and noises I'd made. My pulse thundered in my ears as I sprang forwards again and scuttled to the far wall, then held still.

Baba was on the phone, wearing his headset. He must not have heard me, because he didn't look up. I wasn't surprised. He hardly ever paid attention to me. For once, I was glad.

I released a deep breath of relief, then glanced around the room. It was empty, apart from a half-broken bed frame on one side and a child-sized desk on the other. Grey light seeped through the window. Rain clouds had moved in. Next to the window was a door that led to a small balcony enclosed on all sides by wooden screens with cutout holes the shape of four-leaf clovers.

The cat perched next to the window, staring at me. Its tail twitched again, but I couldn't see any sparkles. I was determined to wait, to see if they reappeared.

I sat down and scooted little by little until I was close enough to touch the cat, then I reached out my hand to scratch its chin. The deep rumble of its purr made its whiskers quiver. It blinked its eyes at me blissfully.

"You finally let me stroke you," I said. "Now look how happy you are."

The cat let out a little miaow as if it agreed. It pitched forwards into my chest, purring as it rubbed against me, then curled up in my lap. Its body warmed my legs. The cat had such extraordinary eyes, I couldn't help feeling like it was trying to say something to me, or that it somehow understood what I was thinking.

"You're trying to pretend you're a normal cat now, but I know better. I saw your tail light up. Twice." As I rubbed behind its ears, I could've sworn I saw it nod and smile.

It was almost as though the cat had planned the whole thing out, as if it had drawn me up here to show me something. Maybe something important.

The cat watched me for a moment, then hopped off my lap and padded over to a loose floorboard on the far side of the room, near the broken bed. It extended its paw into the hole underneath it.

"What is it? You want something in there?"

I hesitated for a moment, wondering if it was a good idea to stick my hand into a dark hole. It probably wasn't. Anything could be in there – spiders, mice, rat skeletons. There was no telling in a house this old. But I'd already risked falling through the floor to follow this cat upstairs, so I thought one more unwise thing wouldn't matter. Also, now I was curious what was inside.

The cat scratched at the hole again and miaowed impatiently.

"Okay. Here goes." Taking a deep breath, I leaned down and reached inside, feeling around on the bottom of the hole. There didn't seem to be anything there. Disappointment began to swell in my chest – and then my fingers bumped against something cold and smooth like glass. I pulled out the object and looked.

It was a blue bottle, and it had a half-peeled label wrapped around it. Something was hidden inside – a rolled-up scrap of paper. Maybe it was an ancient message, or better yet, a treasure map. I thought I'd better have a look.

As I pulled out the cork, a puff of glittering gold dust burst out. Some of it got into my nose, so I sneezed in the crook of my arm, then wiped my eyes and held the bottle close. In old-fashioned, curlicue lettering and faded blue ink, the label read:

Mustafa'nin Sihirli Mürekkep Şişesi

I had no idea what it meant. It had to be Turkish, I guessed, but I couldn't be sure.

Then the words disappeared, and the label went blank. That was impossible. My eyes had to be playing tricks on me.

Slowly, new words began to appear on the label, fresh and wet, one letter at a time, like a secret message being written with an invisible pen:

Mustafa's Magic Ink Bottle

My stomach twisted with excitement. Maybe my eyes *weren't* playing a trick on me. This could be real, just like when I saw the cat's tail sparkle.

I stared at it. The label was in English now, and I could read it, but I still wasn't sure I understood. A *magic* ink bottle?

I stuck my finger into the bottle and fished out the piece of paper that was rolled up inside. It read:

Some like adventure. Some like to roam.
Some want a friend. Some want to go home.

It didn't look like a treasure map. It looked more like a poem or a riddle. I pursed my lips and considered. Whatever this was, it didn't make much sense. I continued reading:

This magic bottle grants a wish,
But it will only give you one.
Rub the magic bottle,
And it will be done.

The bottle granted a wish if I rubbed it? So, a genie would pop out and ask me what I wanted? That was ridiculous. I sniggered to myself, wondering if the whole thing was a joke. Magic didn't exist. Everyone knew that. Besides, wish-granting genies were supposed to live in lamps, not ink bottles. Maybe someone was taping me, like a television programme that played tricks on people just to see what they'd do and then laughed at them when they fell for it.

Still, a shiver of hope rocked my shoulders. What if it wasn't a joke?

I read the end of the rolled-up note, which was written in slightly larger letters:

Your family has a secret,
both strange and true;
Discover the secret, if you so choose.

Zehra Hala had mentioned a family secret and an adventure. Did she know about the cat and the magic bottle? It almost seemed as if the riddle had been written specifically for me, but it couldn't have been – I'd only arrived yesterday. This bottle looked like it had been hidden for years. I shook off the thought. Lots of other families had secrets, and the riddle could've been written for any one of them.

But at the bottom of the yellowed pages was a pen-and-ink drawing of a white cat with different shades of eyes and a black-tipped tail, like the one in front of me.

I put my hand on my hip. "Is this what you brought me here for? A silly bottle and a riddle?"

The cat held my gaze.

"I'm supposed to rub the magic bottle, right?"

It continued to stare at me.

"You aren't very talkative, are you?"

I rolled my eyes at myself. Of course it wasn't talkative. Cats couldn't talk.

I examined the bottle. If it *wasn't* magic – and it probably wasn't – then there'd be no harm in rubbing it. If it *was* magic, then I'd get a wish, which would be good.

I'd read plenty of fairy tales about people finding magic objects – flying carpets and rings of power and bewitched roses and invisibility cloaks – but I'd never really thought about what I would do if I ever found such an object. I tipped my head, my brain whirring. Maybe I should rub it, just to see what happened.

"Dalya!" Baba stood in the doorway, his veins popping on his neck. "What are you doing here? I've been looking everywhere for you!" he bellowed.

I jolted, surprised, my stomach sinking like a rock in water. "I'm sorry – " I tried to find a good excuse but came up with nothing. "I wanted to see the cat," I finished weakly.

"You followed a cat up here?" He gaped at me. "What cat?"

I glanced around the room, but it wasn't there. Maybe it was hiding in the cupboard – Baba must've scared it.

He threw up his hands. "What were you thinking? I specifically told you to stay downstairs."

My eyes stung. He didn't have to yell like that. "But I – "

"I told you it wasn't safe up here," he said. "Come downstairs with me right now!"

There was no arguing with him once his neck veins popped. It was better to stay quiet. I stuffed the yellowed paper and ink bottle into my cardigan pocket and trotted after him. When I got to the staircase, a sad miaow echoed after me. The cat nosed around the corner and watched me leave.

"I'm sorry, but I can't stay," I whispered. "Why don't you come downstairs?" I wasn't sure why I was still talking to it.

"Let's go!" Baba called over his shoulder as his phone buzzed in his pocket. He stopped and put his headset on. "I have another meeting."

"But you said – "

"I know what I said," he snapped.

A flash of electric anger shot through my veins. He'd brought me halfway across the world only to ignore me, just like he always did at home.

He stood at the top of the stairs, furiously poking at his phone.

I glared at him, then grabbed the bottle from my pocket and rubbed it. "I wish I were at home," I whispered.

I hoped I'd suddenly disappear. It'd be better than waiting forever for Baba to be finished with his work. It'd serve him right if I vanished into thin air.

"I did it," I said to the cat. "I rubbed the bottle and made a wish. Now what?"

I waited a moment. Nothing. I rubbed it again, in case I'd done it wrong the first time, but still nothing. I waited some more, then I shook my head.

Magic wasn't real – of course it wasn't. Nobody truly believed in magic except for little kids who didn't know better.

"You almost made me believe," I murmured glumly as I turned on my heels to leave.

It miaowed one last time, but I didn't look back.

Baba led the way, zigzagging down the creaky staircase. When we got to the bottom of the stairs, he stopped and gathered me into a tight hug. He didn't say anything.

I held still, surprised.

"I won't do it again, Baba," I said. "I'll be careful."

"I'm sorry I snapped at you." He gave me a final squeeze.

"I'll get this meeting out of the way and we'll do something together today. I promise." He kissed the top of my head and headed for his room.

As I turned away, I felt a pang of guilt. I'd been gone for less than fifteen minutes and he'd got seriously worried. Who knows what he would've done if I'd disappeared, like I'd hoped? I shut the door and slumped on the bed.

As I reached for my book again, my cardigan pocket rustled. Then it wiggled and quivered like something alive was inside. Maybe a mouse had got into my pocket while I was upstairs. I yelped and slid out of my sweater, then jumped backwards and stared at it, waiting for it to move again.

It didn't move. After a minute, I grabbed a pencil from my suitcase and stepped forwards to prod the pocket. Still nothing. Using the pointy end, I held it open to peer inside. I couldn't see anything except the paper and the ink bottle, only now they were both glowing brightly. The paper crinkled and shivered again.

Carefully and gently, I pulled it out and unrolled it. The riddle in curlicue writing was gone. In its place were the words:

Wish Granted

What did that mean? My wish hadn't been granted – I'd asked to go home.

The drawing of the cat had changed too. I looked closer.

The ink shimmered like it was made of silver. I was sure it had been black. I reached out my finger to touch it – when the drawing at the bottom of the page moved. My breath caught at the top of my throat.

The cat drawing paced back and forth across the paper like a tiny tiger in a paper cage, as if it were alive . . . or *magic*.

I cautiously poked it. It opened its mouth with a tiny roar and jumped to avoid my finger, then it sat down in the left corner and stared directly at me as it swished its tail, releasing a wisp of the same fizzy fairy dust I'd seen before.

I tried to touch the cat drawing again, but it scampered sideways and nipped at me, then sat down and licked its paw.

I yanked my finger back. That nip had hurt. A smudge of ink had got on the tip of my finger where the cat drawing had bitten me. Wincing in pain, I rubbed my thumb over it. The metallic liquid sparkled.

My body began to tingle like a thousand tiny pins pressing into my skin. The air cooled and the room darkened around me. I glanced around, trying to understand what was happening. Everything went blurry, like I'd suddenly fallen into a dream, and a wave of fear swept over me as the walls fell away and vanished into blackness.

I floated in the dark, my body cold and motionless, as if I were suspended in the night sky. I tried to shout as my arms and legs disappeared, but no sound came out. Wisps of gold dust swirled around the last of my fingertips, and then everything went still. The only thing moving was my mind, whirling like the long, slow arms of the Milky Way. I turned and turned until I was woozy, so I focused on a single star, the biggest one I could see, to get my bearings. The star grew and grew, until its light blinded me.

When I opened my eyes again, I was lying in the bright morning sun . . . and I had no idea where I was.

4

THE BLOOD-CURDLING SCREAM

The first thing I noticed was the warmth of the afternoon sun on my face. I blinked and yawned as I opened my eyes and looked around.

I was sprawled on top of a red silk pillow in the middle of a brightly lit room, not much larger than a walk-in wardrobe. Its window was wide and large, and there was a painting of a red tulip on the wall. The room looked familiar, but I couldn't remember exactly when or where I'd seen it.

A cool breeze flowed through the open window. As I took a deep breath, I noticed something interesting: The smells around me were unusually strong. Not in a bad way – it was actually good. The sweet perfume of a rosebush wafted in from the window, and a breeze brought the scent of freshly cut grass. I bent forwards and sniffed the pillow underneath me. It had the soapy sweet fragrance of lavender. I could smell a hundred lovely aromas all at once, and each one was more powerful than the last.

The sounds around me were unusual too – louder and

sharper, like someone had turned up the volume on everything. There was a bird sitting on a tree branch outside, and I could've sworn I heard it breathing. It locked eyes with me, and then took flight.

I squinted at the tree outside. There was something wrong with my eyes. The leaves, the sky and the clouds were all shaped perfectly, but the colours were odd, some brighter than usual and some faded, as if someone had slipped a filter over my eyes.

Actually, my whole body felt weird. I wasn't sick to my stomach, exactly, but then I didn't feel right either. I wasn't dizzy or feverish or travel sick. I was just . . . different.

A lightning bolt of itchiness tickled my nose. I raised my right leg and scratched the itch with my foot –

I froze in horror as I peered down my nose.

I had whiskers. Itchy ones. And I'd scratched them with my foot.

Only my foot wasn't a foot. I had four claws where there should've been toes. My foot was a *paw*.

I held my hands in front of my face, but they were paws too. I twisted to look at my rear end. Was that . . . a *tail*? I spun around and around trying to grab it for a better look, but I couldn't catch it. My arms, my shoulders, my belly – my whole body was covered with *fluffy white fur*. My spine snapped straight as an arrow. I tried to scream but all that came out was a screeching miaow.

I reeled backwards at the terrible sound. I fell sideways and rolled towards the edge of the pillow. Gasping, I teetered on the edge – four paws in the air, sticking out in all directions, my tail puffed – until I totally lost my balance and tumbled off the pillow to the floor with a flump.

I scrambled to four feet and stood perfectly still. This could not be happening. It was absolutely, positively, not real – all I needed to do was calm down.

Forcing myself to breathe, I closed my eyes. When I opened them again, I spotted a wrinkled reflection in the glossy window across the room.

A cat with snow-white fur, shiny whiskers, a pink nose, and blue and gold eyes stared back at me. As I moved my head from side to side, the cat in the window moved along with me. I spun around in a circle, and it spun with me. I stretched my curved hind legs, then hopped on top of the pillow and hopped back down. I extended my claws and dug them into the pillow's fabric, then plucked them back out. I rotated my ears forwards and back one at a time. I wiggled my whiskers, then stuck out my tongue. The reflected cat copied my every move.

There was no doubt about it. I was looking at *my* fur, *my* eyes and *my* whiskers. The black tip of my tail sparkled like it was dipped in twinkling stars. When I swished it, a wisp of golden dust swirled in the air.

Something had happened to me – something strange. Like, off-the-charts strange. On a scale from one to ten, this was eleventy million *strange*.

I had to work out what had happened and why, and I needed to do it quickly. My pulse pounded so hard my whiskers quivered as flashes of memory returned to me: the magic ink bottle, the yellowed paper, the wish. I couldn't remember the exact words of the riddle, but I was pretty sure it hadn't said anything about turning into a cat. If it had, I wouldn't have rubbed the bottle. I'd wanted to go home, not sprout whiskers.

It didn't matter what the riddle said, though, because there was no such thing as magic. It simply couldn't be real. Even if magic *did* exist, which it didn't, my wish hadn't come true.

There was only one explanation: I was dreaming. That had to be it. I considered biting my own tail to wake myself up, but then I remembered that I hadn't been able to catch it when I'd chased it.

I had to admit, I'd never had a dream so vivid before. This was too real, complete with sharp smells and loud sounds. So, maybe it *wasn't* a dream. I could be hallucinating. I'd read a story once about girl who ate a weird cake and imagined she was a hundred feet tall. The apple tea Zehra Hala gave me yesterday might've had an unfamiliar spice in it, and I could be having a bad reaction to it. How would I know?

I shook my head, trying to calm myself. If this was a dream, then there was nothing I could do except wait to wake up, but if I was hallucinating, then maybe Baba could help me. I sprang from the pillow and darted through the doorway to find him, though I wasn't sure how he was going to fix this. Hopefully, he'd tell me I was being silly, and I'd snap out of it. It wasn't much of a plan, but it was all I had.

I was already zipping through the hallway before I realized I had no idea where I was. The hallway ended and the space lit up, leaving me blinded by splashes of sunlight scattering down a polished flight of stairs. At the bottom was a Turkish rug so red it nearly glowed, and a crystal chandelier hung from the centre of the ceiling like a giant glass cake. Shimmering rainbows of light streamed through its dangling prisms and bounced between framed mirrors along the walls.

For a split second my vision doubled – the chandelier was rusted and old, with only two working lightbulbs, and then it was shiny and new again. I stared at the chandelier, blinking and thinking, until it came to me. I knew exactly where I was: the entrance hall of Zehra Hala's old mansion. Only her house wasn't run-down or dusty anymore. Everything looked new, like someone had fixed the place up. But how could that be true? It didn't make sense.

I bounded forwards, desperately hoping Baba was still in his room. My claws made tip-tap noises on the wooden floors as I head-butted the door open.

The room was empty. Baba's luggage was gone, and there was nothing in the wardrobe except extra blankets. I leapt onto the mattress and sniffed the pillow. He always wore designer aftershave, but there wasn't even a whiff of it clinging to the sheets. I scurried across the hall to my own room, but my belongings were missing too.

Baba had to be there somewhere, didn't he? Maybe he'd gone out to do some errands again and he'd be back soon. I sank to the floor to wait, anxiously telling myself that everything would be okay.

As I crouched down, I heard a faint sound, like the clinking of silverware, coming from a nearby room. *Baba*. Getting to my feet, I quickly padded back through the entrance hall and bolted into the dining room, but it was empty. I let out a frustrated growl. Where *was* he?

As I glanced around the room, a heavenly aroma floated past me. I lifted my nose to sniff. It smelled sweet and creamy, and it was coming from the dining room table. My stomach rumbled, reminding me how long it'd been since I'd eaten. I knew I should probably sit down and wait, but the food smelled *so good*. There was no harm in taking a quick look, right?

The dining room table was a high jump, but there was only one way to see what was on top of it, so I coiled my muscles like springs and vaulted into the air, landing with a skidding stop next to a set of tulip-shaped glass teacups. Any more momentum and I'd have kicked the whole set to the floor.

I twitched the whiskers above my eyes, pleasantly surprised I'd managed to make it, then ambled towards the tea set to find a plate with a biscuit on it. Inhaling deeply, I let myself enjoy the smell, then I took a nibble. The biscuit was shaped like a tiny crescent moon and tasted like almonds dusted with icing sugar. It was possibly a bad idea to eat random biscuits without asking, but I was too hungry to hold back. I dived nose-first into the pile of tastiness, scoffing down the whole thing, all the way to the crumbs.

Licking my lips, I glanced around the table, hoping to find something to wash down the biscuit, when I spotted the jug filled with sweet milk. At first I thought I might be able to pick it up with my paws. Sitting back on my haunches, I grabbed the sides, but it kept slipping. *Oh, right,* I thought. *Paws don't have thumbs.*

There had to be a way to drink the milk, though. Cats did it all the time – I'd seen them. But how did they do it? I crouched down, mimicking cats I'd seen drinking milk, positioning myself over the top of the jug. I stuck out my tongue and dipped it into the milk, then I did it again and again. I got a surprisingly large amount of it into my mouth. There was a lot of splashing, though, and I guessed maybe half had landed in my whiskers. Squeezing my face inside the jug, I pushed my nose to the bottom so I could lick up the last delicious drops, then I sat back on my haunches . . . only to realize I couldn't see.

There was something stuck on my head.

It was the jug. I'd shoved my face so far down into the container, I couldn't get it back out again. *Perfect,* I thought. *I'm not just a cat, I'm a brainless one.*

I shook my head back and forth, trying to remove the jug, but it wouldn't budge, so I flopped to my side and wrestled it with my front paws and hind legs, wrenching it until my face popped free and the jug clattered onto the table. I glared at the jug as if it had been the container's fault that I'd got my head stuck inside.

I sat up and was about to clean my whiskers when I spotted something wriggling near the window. For some reason, the way it moved, twitching back and forth, reminded me of

a mouse's tail. A powerful feeling overtook me, an instinct I
didn't recognize. My body tensed, my heart slowed, my eyes
widened, my rear-end waggled. With a sudden explosion of
energy, I launched myself at the wriggling thing and caught
it with my teeth. It was a thread from the curtain. Clamping
down hard, my blood buzzed with wild glee as I clawed the
thick fabric, thumping it with my hind legs and thrashing my
head from side to side until the string came loose. I chewed on
it for a second before I spat it out and continued chomping on
the curtain because it felt nice on my new fangs.

That's when I heard quick, angry footsteps clomping
towards me.

A woman stomped to a halt. She was wearing an expensive-
looking purple dress embroidered with silver thread. Fancy
emerald rings weighed her fingers down. In her hand was a
tulip-shaped glass teacup. She was beautiful in a terrible sort
of way. Her black hair glinted, and her teeth were all perfectly
rectangular, like tiny bone-coloured gravestones.

The woman opened her mouth and released a blood-
curdling scream.

5

THE GIRL WITH THE PEACOCK FEATHER

The woman hurled the teacup at my head, clipping my left whiskers. The cup exploded against the wall.

My ears flattened, and my tail stiffened like a flagpole. I hesitated, paralysed and terrified, trying to think what to do. The woman was blocking the doorway, and there was no other way out. She lifted her hand to fling the saucer. My pulse pounded in my jaw. I didn't care how, I had to get out of there immediately – so I tucked my chin and charged straight at the woman, running between her legs.

I scampered up the steps, my claws scraping and sliding on the polished wood, before I raced through the first open door I could find. I scanned the room, looking for somewhere to hide. My heart skittered like a butterfly in a storm as I dived headfirst under the bed and hid in the darkness.

Who *was* that woman? I couldn't believe she tried to kill me with a teacup just because I was biting her curtains. That seemed like a pretty extreme overreaction, in my opinion. I'd been telling myself I was imagining things, but this felt *real*.

The mattress above me squeaked. My blood chilled. Oh no. Someone else was in the room with me.

A girl with wide hazel eyes edged over the side of the bed and stared at me upside down. She couldn't have been more than twelve years old, the same age as me, but she looked huge, mostly because I had shrunk to the size of a cat. Something about the girl's eyes was familiar, like I'd seen them somewhere before, or they reminded me of someone I knew.

"Can you please turn off your tail?" whispered the girl.

I bunched the whiskers above my eyes, confused. The girl was speaking to me, and I could understand her.

Why was she speaking English? Shouldn't she be speaking Turkish? How could I understand her? Even though everything looked slightly different, this was still Zehra Hala's house, wasn't it? That meant I was in Istanbul, didn't it? Questions crowded my thoughts.

If this was all a dream, then maybe being able to understand everyone, no matter what language they were speaking, was a part of it. I wondered if I'd be able to understand other animals too, like birds and squirrels. Nothing made sense to me anymore, so there was no telling what would happen next.

The girl pointed. "Turn it off, or she'll see you."

My tail was sparkly yellow, lighting up the underside of the bed. I had no idea why it was glowing, and I definitely didn't know how to make it stop.

Fast, furious footsteps neared the door.

I already knew who it was by the sound: the woman who had

thrown the teacup at me. I glanced around frantically, then sank my teeth into a nearby pillow and backed into the corner underneath the bed. As the door swung open, I set the pillow over my tail, snuffing out the glow.

The girl shot to her feet.

Making sure my tail was covered, I crept forwards and crouched down low so I could see what was happening.

The woman blustered into the room. Her black hair gleamed in the sun as she scowled at the girl.

"Where is the cat?" she bellowed. "I saw it come in here!"

As the girl stepped forwards, I got my first good look at her. She was wearing a tattered beige dress with a faded blue scarf tied like a belt around her waist. Her slippers were pointy and curled upwards at the toe, but they were worn and looked like they were a size too small, as if someone had forgotten to buy her a new pair. On her head was a coil of faded pink velvet fabric tied in a swirl. A scraggly old peacock feather drooped from the top of the swirl. She looked like someone dressed up in a shabby costume they'd found at a jumble sale.

The girl was also skinny, with dark circles under her eyes. She shrank back when the woman got close, her bottom lip quivering. She looked so small and scared, I felt sorry for her.

The woman's body rocked with an explosive sneeze.

"Where is it? You know I can't have cats in the house!" roared the woman. "Every single one of those disgusting devils should be tossed in a river." She marched around the room, kicking baskets and loose piles of clothes. She sneezed again and again as she inched closer to me.

Panic squeezed my chest. It was only a matter of seconds before the woman checked under the bed. *She'd see me. She might even toss me in a river.* The fur on the back of my neck rose as I slunk backwards as far as I could.

As she neared the bed, the woman bent at the waist. My whiskers trembled, and I held my breath.

"It's gone!" the girl yelped. "The cat went out the window!"

The woman straightened and whirled around. "It jumped from the first floor?" she said. "That's ridiculous."

The girl fumbled for an answer. "It got scared," she blurted out. "Cats can jump from high places. They always land on their feet. Everyone knows that."

The woman narrowed her eyes to slits at the girl. "You'd better not be lying." She peered out of the window. "If you lie to me, you won't see a scrap of food for three days. Do you hear me?" The woman sneezed again, followed by a wet sniffle. "Air this place out immediately and clean it up. You should be thankful you have a roof over your head. Your father hasn't sent a single piece of gold to feed you. You'd be begging in the streets if it weren't for me."

"Yes, Aunt Sibel. I understand. I wouldn't lie to you."

"My friends are coming over tonight. You are not to come downstairs while my guests are here. Do you hear me? We don't want any children around." Aunt Sibel stabbed a bejewelled finger at the girl. "Especially naughty children like you."

"Yes, Aunt Sibel," said the girl.

"I'm going out to get a few things before my guests arrive. There are cold beans and rice in the kitchen. Eat it before I get back or you won't get supper," she said. "And if I see that cat again, I'll toss you both in a river myself!"

The woman slammed the door behind her. A trailing echo of angry clomps followed her.

I let out my breath, but I was still shaking. Whoever that woman was, she was horrid.

"You can come out now," whispered the girl.

I watched the girl for a moment, debating whether or not I should trust her. She seemed nice enough, and she'd just saved me from an extremely nasty woman, so she was probably safe. It was worth the risk to find out if she knew anything about what was going on.

I crept forwards on my belly, out from underneath the bed, and sat down. I needed to find some way to talk to her, but I had no idea if I'd be able to speak. The last time I'd tried to make a noise, it'd come out as a howling miaow.

I swallowed. "Who–*miaow*," I spluttered, then concentrated. My voice came to me slowly at first, more like a whisper, then it gained strength.

"Who . . . was . . . that?" I asked.

"You can talk! How wonderful," said the girl. "That was Aunt Sibel. My father is a travelling merchant. He's rarely home. So Aunt Sibel is here to take care of me. Actually, I haven't seen my father in five years." A frown eclipsed the girl's smile, but then she brightened again. "But I'm so glad you're here! I didn't think the magic would work, but look at you! You're *real*."

My mind knotted with questions. "You did some kind of magic? *You* did this?"

"Not exactly," said the girl. She set a small glass ink bottle in front of me. The label was blank. Then, words began to appear, fresh and wet, one letter at a time, like a secret message being written with an invisible pen. It said: "MUSTAFA'S MAGIC INK BOTTLE." It looked exactly like the bottle I'd found.

More writing began to appear. Underneath "Mustafa's Magic Ink Bottle", in much smaller writing, it read: "PLEASE RETURN THE BOTTLE TO MUSTAFA THE GREAT, SHOP NUMBER FOURTEEN, FLEA MARKET DOOR, GRAND BAZAAR." What did that mean? Mine hadn't said that, had it? I'd been more concerned with poking the cat drawing than reading the bottle.

"There was a piece of paper inside it." The girl unrolled it and read it out loud:

Some like adventure. Some like to roam.
Some want a friend. Some want to go home.
This magic bottle grants a wish,
But it will only give you one.
Rub the magic bottle,
And it will be done.
Your family has a secret, both strange and true;
Discover the secret, if you so choose.

It was the same riddle I'd found, word for word.

"I wanted a friend, so that's what I wished for. Of course, I hadn't expected a talking cat. The riddle didn't say anything about cats. But I'm so lonely here in this house – Aunt Sibel never lets me have anyone over – and here you are! Isn't it wonderful?" The girl's smile exploded with delight as if this was the best day of her life.

I stared at her, rearranging her words in my head over and over again until I finally understood.

I'd wanted to go home. She'd wanted a friend. We'd both read the riddle and followed the instructions – that's how this had happened. *Magic.* And it had been done to both of us.

Only the bottle hadn't actually granted *my* wish. Instead, it had turned me into a cat, which didn't seem fair at all. If the magic had happened to both of us, then why was only one of us an animal? And why didn't Zehra Hala's house look old and run-down anymore?

I hadn't stopped to think about how the magic worked or how long it might last before I rubbed the bottle. I definitely hadn't considered the possibility of growing a tail.

I just wanted to go home.

I didn't want to be a cat forever. But if I had no idea how the magic worked, then I had no idea how to reverse it. Fear caught in my throat as a list of frightening questions grew in my mind. What if I *never* changed back into a human? What would my mum do if I never came home? What would Baba do?

I was suddenly dizzy. As I collapsed on a pillow, I noticed a door that led to a balcony enclosed on all sides by wooden screens with cutout holes the shape of four-leaf clovers. On one side of the room was a bed with a rumpled blue blanket, and on the other was a child-sized desk littered with papers.

"I've been here before. This is where I found the ink bottle," I wheezed, "but the room was old and dusty."

"Old? Dusty?" The girl huffed. "My family had this house built five years ago. It's nearly new."

She was right: The house looked and smelled new. Even the paint on the walls was fresh.

A shiver shook me from my nose to my tail as the realization dawned on me. If this *was* Zehra Hala's house, and it was built *five years ago*, then it could only mean one thing . . . and it wasn't good.

6

THE WAY HOME

I hadn't thought things could get worse than becoming a cat, but I was wrong. If the girl was telling the truth about the house being built five years ago, that meant I had *gone back in time*.

I looked more closely at the girl standing in front of me. Her hazel eyes seemed familiar to me, like I'd seen her somewhere before, and then it came to me. The old painting in the hallway – the one of a girl with a cat on her lap – this was *her*.

Zehra Hala told me the painting in the hallway was my great-great-grandmother . . . which meant this girl was related to me.

My mind reeled and I felt dizzy again. I'd been thinking I could ask Baba for help, but if I'd gone back in time, then he hadn't been born yet.

My fear soured to anger in the pit of my stomach like rotten milk. I couldn't believe I'd got into this mess. I'd *told* Baba the mansion looked creepy when we first arrived and he'd laughed at me like I was being ridiculous, but I knew something wasn't right about this place. If he hadn't forced me to go to Istanbul for my summer holiday, if he hadn't taken me to that house, if he hadn't broken his promise and hadn't left me alone while he worked, then I wouldn't have followed that stupid cat upstairs, and none of this would have happened. This was his fault.

"I never told you my name," said the girl, interrupting my thoughts. "I'm Mina. Do you have a name? I don't know how this works with magic friends. It would be very nice if I got to name you."

I glared at her, still caught up in my anger at Baba. "I already have a name. It's Dalya."

"Oh, I see." Mina smiled sheepishly. "Do you like to play games, Dalya? My favourite is backgammon. If you don't know how to play the game, I can teach you." Mina hopped up and began digging through her desk. "I have all the pieces here somewhere. I haven't had anyone to play with in ages."

I didn't want to play games. "What year is it?"

"What an odd question. Is this a test?"

"Please tell me."

"It's nineteen hundred and seven." She smiled and leaned forwards. "Did I get it right?"

I felt nauseous. It was one thing to suspect I'd gone back in time. It was another thing to know it for sure. "You have to help me."

"You need my help? How intriguing! Why don't you tell me about it while we play our game." Mina continued rummaging through her drawers, pulling out a wooden board and collecting black and white stones shaped like large coins. "It's lovely to have a friend to talk to. Aunt Sibel only invites her own friends to our house," said Mina. "She loves fancy parties. She has one every night and the music goes on until late at night, sometimes all the way until morning."

That did sound annoying, but I didn't really care about Aunt Sibel's parties. "I'm sorry, but – "

"Oh, there's nothing for you to be sorry about! You're here to save me from my loneliness," exclaimed Mina. "I didn't expect my magic friend to be a cat, but I have to say I like it very much, especially since it bothers Aunt Sibel. Personally, I enjoyed watching her sneeze herself into a fit."

"But I'm not supposed to be a cat," I interrupted.

"What do you mean, you're not supposed to be a cat? Don't be ridiculous. You're perfect the way you are. Don't ever doubt it." Something caught the girl's eye and she reached out to touch it. "Such a pretty collar!"

"What?" I glanced down.

She was looking at the necklace Zehra Hala had given me before I'd gone upstairs. I'd been wearing it when I'd made my wish.

"Yeah, it's great," I said dismissively. "But what I need is – "

"It's lovely! I have a very nice green ribbon we can tie on the pendant and make it look even better," said Mina.

"I don't need – " I protested.

But before I could finish, Mina had whipped out a ribbon from her pocket and then knotted a fancy bow at the base of my neck.

"There! What a pretty kitty you are," said Mina.

"You're not listening to me!" The hair rose on the back of my neck.

Mina's eyebrows knitted together. "Don't you want to be my friend?"

"That's not – "

"Then what is it?" Mina demanded.

Squeezing my eyes shut, I pushed my fears down and quietened my thoughts, one by one. It was terrible that I was alone in this strange place, and it was horrible that I'd somehow been turned into a cat, but I had to focus on finding a way back. I knew what it was like to be lonely – and I felt bad for Mina – but getting home was all that mattered now.

I turned each piece of information I had over like a rock: the riddle, the wish, the bottle.

"Wait a second." I sat up. "You still have it, right? I'll rub the bottle and it'll turn me back."

"Back into what?" asked Mina.

"Give it to me," I demanded, instead of answering her. She handed it over.

"I wish – " I hesitated. The first time I'd rubbed the bottle, I hadn't really thought about it first. This time, I needed to be careful. "I wish I'd never made a wish." That should do it. I rubbed the bottle with my paw and waited. Nothing happened, so I tried again.

"What about the piece of paper, the one with the riddle on it?" I said. "Right before it happened, I saw the drawing move and I touched it. Let me see the riddle."

I clawed at it desperately, but the drawing didn't appear.

"What are you doing? You'll ruin it!"

"It isn't working," I said. "Why isn't it working?"

"What are you talking about?"

"I can't stay like this forever!" I wailed.

Mina eyed me carefully, then sat down. "You seem upset," she said. "Your tail is puffed."

I looked at my tail. Mina was right. On top of everything else, I had no idea how my new body worked. It had taken me almost ten minutes to get a drink of milk out of the jug, and my head had got stuck. I had no idea how my tail worked – how to puff or de-puff it, and how to turn off the crazy sparkles. At some point, I was going to have to work out how to use a litter tray. That was almost certainly going to be interesting in a very bad way.

"I was delighted to find a friend, but you are not delighted at all." Mina's eyes reddened. "I didn't mean to make anyone unhappy."

Mina's shoulders curved downwards like a frown. It wasn't her fault this had happened, but I couldn't stay just to be her friend.

"I know you didn't mean it," I said. "The thing is, I'm not really a cat."

"But . . . if you're not a cat, then what are you?"

"I'm a girl."

Her eyes widened. "The magic bottle turned a girl into a cat? How awful."

I nodded in agreement, then let out a long sigh. There had to be a way – something I wasn't seeing yet.

"I have an idea," I said, hopping to my feet. I remembered the one small difference between her bottle and mine. Hers had something written at the bottom. It was true I'd been transformed into a cat and been transported into the past, but maybe I wasn't entirely alone – maybe there *was* someone who could help me. "Let me see your bottle again."

She put it on the floor in front of me.

I stuck my paw inside and rolled it back and forth, studying it. There it was: "PLEASE RETURN THE BOTTLE TO MUSTAFA THE GREAT, SHOP NUMBER FOURTEEN, FLEA MARKET DOOR, GRAND BAZAAR."

"The Grand Bazaar? What's that?" I asked. "And who's Mustafa the Great?"

"You've never heard of the Grand Bazaar?"

I shook my head. "I'm not from . . . here."

Mina tipped her head at me quizzically, then shrugged. "I don't know anyone named Mustafa the Great, but the Grand Bazaar isn't far."

"The bottle says he's got a shop. Maybe if we find him, he'll be able to change me back." And send me home. A rush of relief washed over me. "You can take me there, right?"

Mina laughed. "Young girls don't leave the house alone. It's simply not done." She shook her head as if I was crazy.

Oh, right. I'd gone back in time. It made sense that girls didn't go out alone to busy markets. My mum hardly let me go to the cinema alone, and Mina couldn't have been much older than me. "What if you were dressed as a boy?" I asked.

"What a silly idea!" she exclaimed.

"You father must've left some clothes here. If you rolled up the trouser legs, or fixed them somehow, they might fit you."

"You're serious, aren't you?" Mina stared at me like I was insane. "I don't think you understand. If anyone catches me outside the house alone, you can't even imagine what sort of trouble I'd get into. Aunt Sibel would not stand for that."

I sat back on my haunches. If I didn't get to the Grand Bazaar, I'd never find my way home. Mina had to help me. After clearing my throat, I spoke firmly. "You rubbed the bottle hoping to find a friend. Here I am. I need your help."

She was silent.

I glared at her, my tail puffing up again. "Real friends help each other. That's what they do. They don't let the people they care about suffer alone. Maybe you don't care about me – that's fine – but if you *want* a friend, you've got to *be* a friend. That's how it works."

Her face fell, so I knew my words had landed in the right place.

"I'm sorry you were turned into a cat." Her voice wavered. "But you're asking too much of me. I can't take you to the Grand Bazaar. It's too dangerous."

She marched to her bed and blew out the oil lamp, then

rolled over with her back to me.

I sat there for a minute, motionless. Mina was the only person I knew, and she was determined not to help. What was I was supposed to do now? Try to find the Grand Bazaar myself? I had no idea how I was going to do that.

I stood up slowly and leapt onto the open windowsill so I could look outside. The trees rustled as a chilly evening breeze fingered its way through my fur. I curled into a ball, wrapping my tail around my body as tightly as I could, trying to get warm. There were a thousand reasons to cry, but all I felt was cold and empty, as if the hopelessness of my situation had hollowed me out.

The sound of laughter from Aunt Sibel's guests arriving filtered upwards from the entrance hall. I raised my nose and sniffed. The air filled with the smell of fancy rosewater perfume.

There was another smell too – one I didn't recognize. I lowered my nose and scanned the courtyard. A shadow crept into a square of window light.

It was a dog, massive and meaty as a lion, with cream-coloured fur and a curly tail. Its nose and ears were tipped with brown and its eyes gleamed like two copper pennies. I sat still, my whiskers and ears straight and alert.

The dog licked its lips hungrily, like it hadn't eaten in weeks. It watched me, silently eyeing the distance to my window, but I was out of reach, at least for now. The dog gave me one last look before it muscled to its feet and turned to leave.

I watched the dog go, then tucked my nose glumly under my paw. I hoped the dog wouldn't be waiting for me when I set out on my journey the next day.

But I had a bad feeling it would be.

7

MUSTAFA'S MAGIC SHOP

I didn't sleep, not even for a minute. The whole night I'd stayed awake, perched on the open windowsill, watching the darkness for shadows and movement. Thankfully, the dog hadn't come back. I let out a jaw-cracking yawn as the sky turned pink with the rising sun.

The courtyard below didn't look anything like it had when I'd followed the cat outside yesterday. Before, the courtyard had been choked with weeds and packed with dead branches, but now everything was sparkling green. Perfectly trimmed lemon trees with waxy leaves followed the front path down to the brick wall with the O-ring door in the middle. The wall was no longer crumbling but instead was brick red and looked new. Star-shaped blue flowers dotted the tidy garden, and insects crowded around each bloom, buzzing with summer business.

Pointy evergreen trees lined the outer fence of the house. The tall blocks of flats that had boxed us in hadn't been built yet, so the view of the clear blue sky was spectacular. Seagulls twirled above the tree line and the air still smelled like salt and fish.

Some colours still looked slightly faded to me, and the sounds still seemed louder than usual, but I was starting to get used to my new cat senses.

"What do you think?"

I leapt straight up in the air, my back arched and my fur sticking out as though I'd been electrocuted. I fell to the ground, my claws scrabbling on the wooden floor until I found my feet. Mina stared at me, surprised.

"I'm sorry. Did I scare you?"

"You shouldn't sneak up on people like that." I'd seen cats get startled before and I remembered thinking it was hilarious, but it was a lot less funny when it happened to me. My blood thundered in my veins.

Taking a deep breath, I tried to calm myself. I smoothed my tail with my paw, using my claws like a comb, before I glanced up at Mina. She was wearing a long white shirt and blue waistcoat, along with a pair of ridiculously baggy striped trousers with the bottoms rolled up. On her head was a maroon hat shaped like an upside-down saucepan without a handle. Its silky silver tassel dangled past the bottom of her ear.

"You're staring. Do I look silly?"

Actually, she looked *extremely* silly, but I didn't care. If she was dressed as a boy, it meant she was going to take me to the Grand Bazaar. "You're going to help me?"

"Yes." Mina lowered her eyes. "I'm sorry I wasn't a good

friend last night. I don't have much practice. Are you angry with me?"

If I could've hugged her, I would've. A burst of relief swelled in my chest. We would find Mustafa together! As I lunged forwards and rubbed past her leg, a rumbling purr erupted in my throat, which tickled in a nice way.

She patted my back gently. "We should get going. Whenever Aunt Sibel has a party, she sleeps the whole next day. She won't be awake until it's nearly evening."

Mina took off her slippers and quietly slipped out of her bedroom door, then gestured for me to follow. We turned the corner and crept past the top of the stairs, then across to the closed door. Mina put her ear against it, listening. Carefully, slowly, she opened the door and we peeked inside the room. Aunt Sibel was sprawled on a pile of red silk pillows, snoring loudly, her arms and legs stretched wide like an overgrown starfish.

It looked like Aunt Sibel had hosted the party in her room. Dirty teacups covered the table. Half-eaten cinnamon biscuits littered the floor. Fatty meat sauces pooled on stacked plates. I lifted my nose and sniffed. The meat – that was what had smelled so tasty the night before.

Mina pressed her fingers to her lips. "*Shh.* We have to tiptoe past her."

"Okay." I wasn't sure how cats were supposed to tiptoe, but I was willing to give it a try.

Mina pointed. "We need to go through the window on

the far side of the room, hang on to the ivy vines, and climb down the side of the house."

"Wait. What? There's a door downstairs."

"Aunt Sibel locks the doors and keeps the key on a chain around her neck, but she always forgets to lock the window next to her balcony."

The window was pretty high up. Climbing down the side of a house sounded dangerous. "So, I'm guessing you've done this before?"

"Oh no! I would never," said Mina.

"Then how do you know it'll work?"

Mina shook her head. "I don't."

I blinked at her. Everything about this plan seemed like a bad idea, but if we wanted to get out of the house – if I didn't want to live the rest of my life as a cat – then we didn't have much choice. "Let's do it."

Mina crept across the room, picked up a stool, and placed it underneath the window. She reached up to unlatch it. As she pushed it open, it let out a squeak.

Aunt Sibel snorted loudly. Mina and I froze, our eyes glued to her. Aunt Sibel let out a sniffling grunt as she rolled on to her side, and the rolling snores started again. Mina's shoulders relaxed, and she turned back to the window. She peeked out, then hoisted herself up onto the ledge and swung one leg over the side as she dug her fingers into the vines that crept down the side of the house to the ground below. She tugged on them to see if they'd hold, then pulled herself out of the window.

As I waited for Mina to reach the ground, I noticed a tower of plates next to me. A single slice of meat dangled tantalizingly from between two of them. I knew I shouldn't be thinking about food, but the meat looked so good – dripping with barbecued juices and slathered with sweet apricot sauce. My stomach rumbled like thunder. Before I could stop myself, my tongue flew out to taste a drop of sauce. Hunger rushed to my mouth as I salivated.

One bite couldn't hurt, right? I was *so hungry*.

I put my paws on the window ledge and glanced down to check Mina's progress, then spun back to the stack of plates. Reaching out my paw, a single claw extended, I tugged gently at the piece of meat. It slid out a little as the plates teetered dangerously.

"Dalya? Are you coming?" Mina said from outside, below.

I had to go. Sinking my teeth into the meat, I gave it a quick yank. It slipped into my mouth and I gobbled it up . . . just before the plates toppled with a crash.

A sudden shout echoed in the room.

Aunt Sibel sat straight up. As she locked eyes with me, a lightning bolt of fear ripped through my body.

Oh no.

Aunt Sibel rocketed forwards, snatching at my tail. I scampered towards the window, my claws ripping at the polished floors, but she cut me off. Skidding sideways, I searched frantically for a way out. Before I could find anything, she lunged for me and caught a fistful of fur. I bit her hand and wriggled away, then ran for the only open door I could see – until I screeched to a halt at a dead end.

Behind the door was a broom cupboard, not an exit.

Only it wasn't filled with brooms. Gold and silver coins, hundreds of them, overflowed from shipping crates like a pirate's treasure trove.

But that wasn't all. Dozens of colourful dresses lined the hanging rail. All of them were child-sized, like they'd been tailor-made for Mina. A box on the other side of the cupboard was filled with toys – dolls, musical instruments, miniature chairs, piles of pretty shoes with satin tassels.

It didn't make sense. Mina's clothes were all raggedy and old. Why didn't she wear the nice dresses in here?

Behind me, Aunt Sibel rocked with a terrible sneeze, then shook it off. "I'm going to get you!"

I bolted out of the cupboard and ran for the open window – it was my only hope for an escape. If I wanted to get away, I needed to climb down the vines, but the chair Mina had used had been knocked over, and the windowsill was too high for me to reach. There was only one thing to do: jump. I'd made it onto the dining room table. I could do this.

Probably.

Aunt Sibel raged forwards with a shriek.

I crouched down, focused my vision, flexed my claws, coiled my muscles, and catapulted into the air. Aunt Sibel swooped down to grab me, but I was already airborne. I yowled with glee . . . until I looked down.

I'd missed the windowsill and was sailing straight through the window into the open air. Time seemed to stop for a moment. I sucked in my breath, then plunged downwards, somersaulting nose over tail, my tail spinning wildly.

My thoughts tumbled together. *I can't believe it. This is how it ends. I'm going to end up splattered on the ground like a water balloon.*

Just before I crashed, instinct took over. My spine twisted, my body turned, and *I landed on four feet.*

I crouched there for a second, my eyes startled wide. I wasn't splattered on the ground. Somehow, my cat body had known what to do, all by itself.

"What happened in there?" Mina demanded.

I couldn't shake my surprise. "I'm sorry – did you see that? I landed on four feet."

"Of course you did. You're a cat!"

"But – but – "

The back door of the house banged open. Aunt Sibel's face scorched with rage as she shouted at me. "You filthy cat!" She turned to see Mina. "What are you doing outside? You wicked child!"

Her arm shot out to grab Mina's collar, but Mina swerved sideways.

"Come back here!" Aunt Sibel screeched.

Mina ran, but Aunt Sibel was quick.

I watched them, frantically trying to think of a way to help Mina. If I were my normal size, I could try pushing her from behind, but I was barely ankle-high on her.

Wait. Her ankles – that was it. I raced forwards and swished between Aunt Sibel's legs.

"Get out of here! *Shoo! Shoo!*" she shrieked.

As she raised her foot to stomp on me, I locked my teeth on her ankle. She screamed as she lost her footing and careened to the ground with a thud.

"Let's go!" Mina shouted at me. The two of us dashed down the hill, running as fast as we could, until the house was out of sight.

We stopped to catch our breath under a minty eucalyptus tree. A breeze kicked up the smell of salty air from the sea below. I was surprised by the amount of green that surrounded the city. There were miles and miles of it, making Istanbul look like a stone oasis in a world of wilderness. This was the first good look I'd got of the city. I let my gaze linger over its shapes and colours. A hundred orange clay roofs jumbled together in a chaos of crooked streets. Between buildings, skinny evergreen trees poked at the sky like overgrown fingers. Below us, at the bottom of the hill, a blue bay sparkled with sunlit waves. A horn-shaped inlet of water curved around the base of the hill, and a narrow bridge extended over it.

Mina pointed to a tall structure that looked like a lone castle turret with a cone-shaped hat.

"There's Galata Tower," said Mina. "The Grand Bazaar is crowded. If we get separated somehow, we'll meet there."

I was still taking in the scenery, but I turned to face Mina. "Do you think Aunt Sibel followed us?"

Mina peered uneasily over her shoulder. "I hope not. We should keep moving, just in case."

"What's going to happen when you go back?" I asked.

She shrugged.

My stomach soured. It was all my fault Mina was going to get into trouble. If I'd left the meat alone, Aunt Sibel wouldn't have woken up. "I'm sorry, Mina."

"Don't be. Aunt Sibel would probably be happy if I ran away. She hates taking care of me, but she's the only family I have left, except my father."

"Why don't you tell your dad? You could ask him to come home."

"He wouldn't care. If he had, he would've sent money so Aunt Sibel could take care of me. Actually, it would serve him right if I disappeared." Her eyes reddened.

Her words surprised me, mostly because I remembered thinking the exact same thing right before I rubbed the ink bottle. I wanted to say something nice to make her feel better.

"My dad works all the time too," I said.

"Does he travel? Is he gone all the time?" she asked.

"No, it's worse. He's there, but he never pays attention to me. Never."

We were both quiet. Mina probably wanted to cheer me up in return, but neither of us could think of anything. As we stood in silence, my mind flashed back to Aunt Sibel's broom cupboard and a shadow of a question formed.

"Are you sure your dad hasn't sent anything for you? What

about all the stuff in Aunt Sibel's cupboard?" I asked.

"What stuff?"

"There were dresses and shoes. You haven't seen them? Everything looked like it was your size. There were toys too, and a lot of silver and gold coins. Most of it was sitting in boxes."

"She had dresses in my size?" asked Mina.

"A lot of them," I said.

"And shoes? And toys?"

I nodded.

"I don't understand."

"Didn't you say your dad was a merchant? Maybe he sent that stuff for you."

"Why would she hide his gifts from me? Why wouldn't she tell me?"

I shook my head. "I don't know."

Mina scowled, her brow wrinkled in thought.

As I watched her, a thatch of weeds between the cobbles caught my attention. Without thinking, I bit down on one of the reeds and began to chew. It tasted fresh and earthy, but its texture was stringy and tickled my throat. I grimaced and hacked up a half-chewed green blob.

"Ew. Why did I eat that?" I mumbled to myself disbelievingly.

"Most of the cats around here eat that stuff. It's just something they do," Mina said.

I cocked my ears at her, thinking. Eating grass had to be a natural instinct, like landing on all four feet. The truth was, I could kind of understand why cats did it. My stomach was sour before and now it wasn't. Still, it was gross. I swiped a paw across my whiskers to make sure there weren't any green bits left around my mouth and made a mental note to avoid eating weeds again, if I could help it.

Mina shook off her scowl and patted me on the head. "Let's find Mustafa the Great. Then we can worry about Aunt Sibel."

As we made our way down the hill, the buildings grew closer together until they formed rows on both sides of the street. Women in long dresses, all of them clutching baskets, crowded around bakeries. Most of them wore scarves over their heads, wrapped like turbans or pinned under their chins. Outside the shops, bearded men sat on low stools, drinking tea from glass cups and puffing on tobacco pipes as long as walking canes. A grey-haired man ambled down the street balancing a platter of bread on his head. Several chickens wandered out from an alley, followed closely by a boy wearing a striped shirt. He scooped the birds up and tucked them under his arm.

I could feel my brain overloading again, just like it had when I'd opened the door to the courtyard to peek out before I turned into a cat. It was a bustling city with lots to look at, all at once, but this time there weren't any cars, lorries or buses. Nothing familiar. It felt like watching an old-fashioned black-and-white film.

"Are you all right?"

I hadn't realized it, but I'd stopped moving. I glanced up at Mina but didn't know what to say. I wasn't okay, not even a little bit, but we had to get to the Grand Bazaar and find Mustafa, or

I was never going to get home.

"I'll be fine," I lied. I wasn't actually sure this was true, but I told myself it was. Taking a deep breath, I forced myself to keep going.

We made our way across a bridge, then huffed up a hill on the other side. We weaved down one street after another until we came to a brick gate with a wide opening shaped like an upside-down U.

It opened onto a dimly lit passageway crowded with shoppers. Shops on both sides were crammed next to each other. One overflowed with stacks of elaborately patterned Turkish rugs. Another had rows of blue-and-white ceramic plates. A third had strings of glittering gold bracelets. Not a single inch went unused. Oil lamps dangled from shiny brass chains attached to the arched ceiling, casting more light than seemed possible.

I'd never seen that much gold, copper, silver and glass in one place. It was as if someone had gathered all the delicately crafted sparkly beautiful things in the world and stuffed them into an oversized jewellery box that stretched as far as I could see. It was breathtaking.

People pushed coins at each other, buying and selling, haggling in heated voices. Some gathered around a stone fountain in the centre of the passageway, using copper cups to catch a drink. A hundred voices roared in my ears, louder than anything I'd ever heard. I blinked, dazed by the sights and sounds, trying to work out which way to go.

The main passageway split into a dozen more passageways, like a maze. I could see why Mina was worried about getting separated.

"Do you see his shop? Do you?" I bolted to the top of Mina's head, excited about the idea of going home.

"Ouch! Careful with those claws." She pulled me off her head and held me under her arm, gripping the ink bottle in her other hand.

"We're looking for shop number fourteen," she said.

Above each shop was a square stone with a number carved into it.

My pulse pounded in my neck. We passed shop number ten on one side of the passage, then shop eleven on the other side, then shop twelve, then shop thirteen. I tried hard to keep calm, but I couldn't. This next one – it had to be Mustafa's shop.

"This is it!" I shouted.

My smile crashed to a frown. We were standing in front of shop number fourteen . . . and it was empty.

8
THE MAGIC RAT

Mustafa the Great's shop wasn't just empty – it was *abandoned*. Cobwebs curtained the walls and mildew soured the air. The shops around it bustled with activity, but the dust in Mustafa's shop looked years deep. There was no telling how long it had been since anyone had set foot inside his shop.

Where was he?

Growing terror climbed the back of my throat as I padded to the back of the shop, hoping to find some kind of clue or anything that might tell us what to do or where to go. "The bottle says we're supposed to return it to his shop. What are we going to do?"

A chirp echoed from across the passageway. I glanced up. Six husky brown squirrels hid in the shadows across from us. They stood unnaturally still, their piercing stares hooked on me.

I leaned sideways and whispered to Mina. "We're being watched."

"What?"

I pointed a claw at the squirrels. "They look mean."

"Don't be silly. They're just squirrels."

Something bothered me about them, but I couldn't put my finger – or even my paw – on it. "Keep your eye on them." As I turned back to hunt for clues, I heard someone speaking. I twisted my triangle ears around to pinpoint the direction. The voice sounded like it was coming from *inside* the wall.

"Wait. *Shh*. Did you hear that?" I asked Mina, automatically cocking my ears.

I got low on my belly and crept towards the wall at the back of the shop. The wall looked thick and old, made of both stone and brick, as if the builders got bored using one material and randomly decided to toss in the other. In the far corner, underneath a wide table, behind a wooden box, along the outside wall, was a loose stone.

The sounds were coming from behind it.

I stared at it, trying to understand, when the stone suddenly opened outwards like a cabinet-sized door, and a rat scurried out. But this wasn't just any rat – this one was wearing a jacket and carrying a tiny shopping bag. It stumbled over a pebble and lost its shoe, then stopped to grab it.

I shook my head, puzzled. The rat was wearing *clothes*?

The rat bent down to tie his shoelaces, mumbling to himself. "Stupid shoes! Now I'm going to be late!"

I rubbed my eyes with the backs of my paws. The rat

was *talking* – and I could understand him, just like I could understand Mina. I'd seen a lot of weird things in the last few days – and everything kept getting weirder.

The rat gathered his things and disappeared behind the stone door.

I held still, thinking. If I could understand the rat, and he could talk to me, then I could ask him about Mustafa the Great. The rat might know something useful. Or, he might not. It was worth trying, though.

"What are you doing?" asked Mina.

"Wait here," I said. "I think I might've found someone who could help."

The door began to close. Just before it did, I stuck my paw inside and nosed through to take a peek. The opening was larger than I expected, and I slipped inside easily. Then I stopped, surprised.

Inside was a miniature replica of the Grand Bazaar – a *rat bazaar* – perfectly sized for rodent shoppers.

Along the sides were shops crammed with tiny Turkish rugs, tiny decorative lanterns, tiny ceramic plates, tiny gold bracelets, tiny patterned scarves and tiny tulip-shaped teacups. Thumb-sized oil lamps hung from brass chains, and the place was packed . . . with *rats*. All of them were dressed. They even had a pinecone-sized fountain in the middle of the passageway where some of the rats dipped their cups for a quick drink of water.

The rat shoppers talked excitedly about the prices of rugs

and copper teapots. A few nibbled on packets of sunflower seeds they'd bought off a wallet-sized cart. I craned my head around to look. The passageway split into a maze that followed the wall.

A peculiar feeling tickled my chest. It was the same one I'd had when I'd seen the loose thread jiggling on the curtain. My muscles tensed. My eyes widened. My hearing sharpened. This had to be some kind of animal instinct. It had helped me land on my feet when I flew through the window, but it probably also made me want to bite anything that wriggled.

I moved myself behind a bit of decorative greenery. I wanted to look at the rats, but I had a feeling the sight of a cat would send them running.

I blinked, trying to take it all in. I'd heard rats were smart and could be trained to do almost anything, but this was amazing.

"*Booooo!*" A chorus of squeaks rang out.

I followed the sound to a shoebox-sized stage. A grey rat with pink ears and pink paws stood on top of the stage. He was dressed in a long black coat and a pointy hat shaped like an upside-down ice cream cone. Chains crisscrossed his chest. A lock the size of a penny hung in the middle. Above him, a sign read "Boz's Famous Magic Show!".

The crowd *booed* loudly again.

"Wait!" said the rat on the stage. "Let me try again!" He fell to his knees, twisting and wriggling as he tried to escape from the chains.

"You don't even know how to do this trick!" screeched one

of the rats in the crowd. "You're a fake!"

"He's no magician!"

"I want my money back!"

The crowd began to leave. The pointy-hatted rat jumped in front of them, trying to stop them. "Give me one more chance. Please!"

But no one listened. As soon as the audience was gone, the rat climbed down off the stage and slumped to the floor next to the decorative greenery where I was hiding. His chest heaved in jagged breaths as tears slid off his whiskers. He pulled a handkerchief from his jacket and gave a wet blow.

As I watched him, the tickling feeling I'd had earlier came back. I crept forwards and away from my hiding place, slowly getting closer to him as the feeling grew.

When his eyes connected with mine, he froze. "Are you going to eat me?" His voice quivered.

The rat's voice startled me out of my trance. "What?"

"It's okay. I deserve to get eaten. I'm a *failure*. But make it quick. I don't want to suffer!" he wailed.

I stepped back. "I'm not going to eat you."

His shoulders quivered as another tear rolled off the tip of his whiskers. "You're not?"

It had been a while since I'd had the biscuits and milk, so I was definitely hungry, but there was no way I was going to eat a rat.

Yuck.

"Ew." I coughed in disgust, then caught the look in his eye.

"No offence," I added.

"None taken." He sighed and shrugged. "I don't blame you for not wanting to eat me. You probably don't even want to be seen with me. I can't even do one lousy magic trick." The rat squirmed over to his jacket and pulled out a key the size of a grain of rice. "I'm supposed to be able to get out of these chains without unlocking them. The trick is to slip the key into the lock without anyone seeing you do it. I've never done it right, though, not once." He sighed as he turned the key and removed the chains, then stuffed them into his hat.

I wasn't sure how to respond to that, so I decided instead to blurt out my question. "Have you heard of Mustafa the Great?"

"Don't you think we should introduce ourselves before we start asking each other questions? I may not be a good magician, but at least I'm polite." He treated me to an elaborate bow. "My name is Boz."

"My name is Dalya." As I offered a smile, I caught him staring nervously at my teeth. I quickly closed my lips. "So, do you know Mustafa?"

"I might. Why do you ask?" He stood up and gathered his things before he made his way back towards the door into Mustafa the Great's shop, and I followed him.

As soon as he got through the door, he jolted to a stop with a squeak. "A human!" he shouted.

"Don't be scared," I said. "This is Mina. She's my friend."

Mina gaped at him, then smiled widely. "A trained rat! And

he can talk? How wonderful. First I make friends with a cat – and now a rat. This has been a very interesting day."

Boz frowned at her, his tone suddenly sharp. "What's so surprising about a talking rat? All rats talk. It's just that humans don't usually listen. They're too busy setting traps for us."

Mina placed a hand over her heart. "I am never too busy to listen."

"That's good to know. If I'm ever caught in a trap, we can have a chat," he said sarcastically. "It was lovely to meet you two, but I have to go home and practise for tonight's show." He gave Mina one last suspicious glance, then turned to leave.

"Wait. You said you might know something about Mustafa the Great. He owns this shop. Do you know where he is?"

"I did say that." Boz eyed me narrowly like he was thinking up a scheme. "But I'm so hungry, it's hard to think." His nose wiggled as he leaned forwards to sniff Mina's pocket. "Is that bread I smell?"

I glanced at Mina, who nodded. "Yes. I brought a small snack," she said. She handed the hunk of bread to him.

Boz hesitated, eyeing Mina. He cautiously reached out a paw and took it from her, then eagerly stuffed it into his mouth. "I can't tell you how much this means to me," he said between mouthfuls.

"Tell us about Mustafa," I said. "The bottle says we're supposed to return it to him, but he isn't here."

"Yes, yes. I'll tell you everything. He's – " Boz was about to take a nibble of bread when his whiskers quivered.

"What?" I said.

He pointed behind me, where six shadows were growing. Mina and I spun around at the same time. The squirrels had us cornered at the back of the shop. They climbed on one another's shoulders in a pyramid stack with the biggest one at the top.

The big squirrel had a dark spot over his top lip that looked like a mustache. He snarled at us, and the squirrels underneath him did the same. "Give us the kitty and no one gets hurt." His voice was raspy and deep.

Squirrels could talk too? I shouldn't have been surprised, given everything that had happened that day, but I couldn't help it. They were *talking squirrels*.

"You were right. The squirrels *do* look mean," Mina whispered to me. "They sound mean too."

The big squirrel growled. "Give us the kitty now."

Mina and I exchanged confused glances. "Are you talking about me?" I asked.

He snorted at me in response, then turned to Mina. "Your Turkish Angora kitty is beautiful. Perfect white fur, one blue eye and one yellow. Very rare. She'd make a good breeder. I believe we'll get a good price for her at the cat bazaar. This is your down payment." He held up a gold coin for Mina to see.

"Once we sell the kitty, I'll give you more gold."

"You want to *sell* me?" I demanded.

He ignored me again, speaking only to Mina. "Tell us

how much you want for her. I will give you money, but we are taking the kitty."

The hair on the back of my neck prickled. "This is ridiculous. You can't kidnap me!"

"Who's going to stop us? Your quivering little rat friend?" asked the big one.

Boz's whole body was trembling. "I'm not s-s-scared."

"Enough stalling," growled a squirrel. "Hand her over."

Mina picked me up and edged along the wall towards the exit. "This cat is not for sale. You can't take her. She is my friend and I'm not selling her to anyone. We are leaving now. Goodbye."

Boz edged along behind Mina. "Yeah! You tell them!" he said from behind her leg.

"We were hoping to do this the easy way, but we can do it the hard way, if you'd like." The big one chirped and the whole stack bared their razor-shape teeth in unison.

"We have to get out of here. *Now,*" I whispered.

The squirrels stretched their claws like they were warming up.

Mina checked over her shoulder. The exit was right behind her. She whirled on her heel and darted forwards.

"*Attack!*" the big one shrieked.

The squirrels flew at her, teeth bared. The big one knocked me out of Mina's hands as her hat tipped backwards and fell off. Then he leapt on her head, tangling his feet in her hair and baring his sharp teeth.

I knew I should've reacted right away, but everything felt like it was going in slow motion. Rage pooled in my stomach as the fur on the back of my neck stood up like a porcupine's. Without thinking, I pulled back my lips, exposed my fangs, and hissed.

The squirrel reeled at the sound. I reeled too, surprised at myself. *I'd just hissed.* And he looked scared for a split second. It was marvellous. I took a deep breath and did it again, this time louder. A wild noise erupted from my throat.

The squirrel tumbled backwards – but another one was already scaling Mina's arm. I had to do something. Hissing wasn't enough. I coiled my muscles and set my eyes on the squirrel.

As he was about to bite Mina's ear, I launched myself from the floor straight up like an arrow and sank my claws into his neck. He yelped and let her go as I dropped back to the floor, punching him with my paws on the way down. As he got back to his feet, Mina and I rushed for the exit, but the other two lunged for me.

"This way!" shouted Boz.

He opened the door to the Rat Bazaar. Mina dropped to her knees. The small door was hardly larger than a cabinet.

"I don't think I'll fit!" she said.

The squirrels all chirped at once as they ran for us.

"Go!" I shoved her from behind. As she squeezed inside, the bottle fell from her pocket.

"Oh!" Mina shouted.

I kicked the bottle to her, and she snatched it up, quickly stuffing it into her waistcoat.

Boz whirled around and tried to shut the door behind us, but the squirrels were fast. The big one already had his head and arm through the door. I kicked him with my back paws, thumping him on the head.

"Does this door have a lock?" I shouted.

"Yes! Get his feet out of the way!" said Boz.

I bit the squirrel's nose. He shrieked. As he pulled back, I gave him a final thwack with my tail, and he lost his grip. Boz leapt forwards and twisted the lock. The squirrels pounded against the door, screaming in anger.

"This way," said Boz. "Come on!"

Squeaky screeches rose from the rat shoppers as they scattered frantically. Mina scuttled forwards on all fours, barely able to fit through the narrow passageway.

Boz took a left and then a right, leading us through the maze, until he got to another door. He pulled it open and pointed across a passageway bustling with men and women. "The exit to the Human Bazaar is right over there."

"The *Human* Bazaar?" asked Mina.

"That's what we call it. Our market is the Rat Bazaar, and your market is the Human Bazaar. There's a Cat Bazaar and a Dog Bazaar too. Humans aren't the only ones with shopping needs," he said. "Now, if we can get out to the street, I'm pretty sure we can lose the squirrels."

He poked his nose out, checking to make sure the coast was

clear. He motioned for us to follow him. We crept through the door into what smelled like a spice shop. The shop was empty, and the exit was just a few feet away.

"Everyone ready?" asked Boz.

Mina and I nodded.

I took a deep breath. Boz scurried out from between two spice baskets towards the exit. Mina and I bounded out after him. We were almost at the door when we heard a loud chirp. One of the squirrels rounded the corner and spotted us. The squirrel chirped again.

"Hide!" I hissed.

"There's an empty basket!" Mina pointed to the corner. Boz and I followed her to the barrel-sized basket and hopped inside, cramming together in a jumble. Mina yanked the wicker top over us.

Mina smothered a cry of pain as Boz's feet dug into her cheek. I was busy trying to breathe with Mina's kneecap squashing my ribcage. Boz's whiskers wriggled like he was going to sneeze when my tail tickled his nose.

"Everyone stop moving," I whispered.

I peeked through the basket's wicker weave. The big squirrel was inside the shop now, and he was looking for us. He threw open the first basket lid. By the smell of it, he'd found cinnamon. He threw open another basket. That one had to be mint. Then another lid and another, until ours was the only one left in the shop. My blood pounded, and Mina choked back a whimper.

The squirrel bared his jagged teeth in an angry snarl as he reached to open our basket's lid.

Just then, the shop owner walked through the door holding a box. "*Shoo! Shoo!*" he yelped at the squirrel. "Get out of my shop! Shoo!"

The squirrel stayed put.

The shop owner grabbed a few hazelnuts from his pocket and tossed them in front of the squirrel. The squirrel's eyes went wide like he was in a trance as he pounced on the nuts and vanished into the hallway.

"Works every time," mumbled the shop owner.

We let out a collective sigh of relief . . . right before the man picked up our basket. Mina's arms pressed down on my tail as we jostled inside the basket.

"What's going on?" whispered Mina.

"I don't know." I took another peek through the basket weave. The man had loaded our basket, along with two other baskets, onto a horse-drawn cart outside the Grand Bazaar exit.

I could see the big squirrel hovering in the doorway to the Grand Bazaar, his oily black eyes searching the area. His gaze fastened on our basket and my breath caught in my throat. He'd found us.

The squirrel chirped and pointed at us as three squirrels gathered behind him. They darted into the crowd, dodging and weaving between legs, racing towards the cart, teeth bared, as the crack of a whip sounded.

The cart lurched forwards onto the bumpy road. With

a second whip crack, the horse took off at a trot. I held my breath. The squirrels rushed through the crowds but couldn't keep up with the horse's pace.

The cart turned left at the junction, leaving the squirrels behind. My stomach unknotted for a moment, then knotted up again. We'd escaped the squirrels . . . but where were we going?

9

THE GOLD-CROWNED PIGEON

"Does anyone have any idea where we're going?" I asked.

My nose pressed into the wicker. I had cramps in both hind legs from being scrunched. I could still see out of the basket with my left eye, though, so I tried to get a look around. We were on a busy street crowded with people selling plums, watermelons and peaches from rickety carts.

I couldn't tell if the squeezing sensation in my chest was distress or Mina's arm in my ribs. It was bad enough I hadn't found Mustafa. Instead, I'd been attacked by a gang of evil squirrels, and now I was stuck in a basket going who knows where. All I'd wanted was to go home, but somehow my wish had backfired and turned into something completely awful.

One step at a time. Taking a deep breath, I reminded myself to focus. We needed to work out where we were going next. Waiting to find out didn't seem like a good idea.

"I say we jump out and make a run for it," I said.

"In the middle of a crowded street?" asked Boz. "You know how humans feel about rats, right?"

"I lost my hat in the stall. Everyone will see I'm a girl. We should wait until we find a place where there are fewer people," said Mina.

Boz snorted. "You're a *girl*? What are you doing on the streets alone?"

"I don't think *rats* should be judgmental," snapped Mina.

The clip-clop of the horse's hooves slowed. "We're stopping. Does anyone recognize this place?" Through a small hole in the basket, I glimpsed a gate flanked by two castle towers.

"It's Topkapi Palace," said Mina.

"Well," said Boz, "you wanted a place with fewer people. There are certainly fewer people inside a royal palace. Too bad most of them are guards armed with swords and trained to catch intruders."

"Swords?" I asked.

"You know, sharp metal things that slice people open?"

"I know what a sword is." I snorted to hide the fact that my throat was starting to pinch shut. Everywhere I looked, there were guards wearing hats that looked like folded napkins. And they had swords. Big ones.

"Those guards are there to keep us out," said Boz.

"But we're already inside," I said.

"Now you see the problem," said Boz.

I did. And I had zero interest in getting my whiskers chopped off. "What are we going to do?" I asked.

The cart halted. The two men in front hopped down,

picked up the baskets around us, hefted them up onto their shoulders, and shuffled through a door.

Boz wriggled to the top of our heap and peeked out from under the lid. "There's no one around. Let's run for that bush."

He pointed his paw over my shoulder. I turned to see a tangled wall of rosebushes lining the palace courtyard. The bush had to be taller than Mina. I didn't know they could grow that high.

"Then what?" asked Mina.

"Try not to get caught," said Boz.

"That's not a solid plan." Mina's voice quivered.

"At some point, someone is going to open this basket and be very unhappy about its contents, as one of us is technically vermin. I don't want to be around when that happens." Boz pushed the basket top off and jumped out. Darting across the cobblestone path, he disappeared through a small opening in the thick jumble of rosebushes.

He was right, and I knew it. If we stayed in the basket, we'd definitely get caught. I climbed up to the edge. "Come on," I whispered to Mina.

She nodded and began to clamber out of the basket, then stopped and tugged on her waistcoat.

"What are you doing?" I said.

"My button is caught on something."

I pricked up my cat ears, swivelling them forwards and sideways. The men were laughing, and the sound was getting closer. "Hurry. They're coming back."

Then I heard a chirp.

Somehow the squirrels from the Grand Bazaar had tracked us. I'd been so worried about where the cart was going, I hadn't stopped to check if the squirrels were following us. It must've taken them a while to catch up, since they were just now making their way through the gate, but if we didn't hide right now, they'd see us. I glanced around frantically as the big one lifted his nose to sniff the air and turned his head in my direction.

"Let's go!" I yanked on Mina's waistcoat as three buttons popped off. She jumped out of the basket. We bolted across the cobblestone path and shot into the rosebushes.

Diving forwards, I braced myself for thorny branches, but there was no need. From the outside, the bushes looked like a wall of leaves, but inside it was hollow, like a secret hideaway. A round tunnel led to the right. Streaks of sunlight lit the mossy ground, giving everything a green glow.

The three of us exchanged looks, silently making sure everyone was okay and accounted for, then we sneaked a quick look to see if the squirrels had spotted us. The big one was out of sight, but I knew he was still searching for us. The two men returned to the cart, gave the horse a crack of the whip, and clip-clopped away.

As soon as it was quiet, I glanced around. On the upside, nobody had attacked us with a sword. On the downside, we were stuck inside a bush. "What is this place?" I asked.

"It looks like some kind of hidden path," said Mina.

"Yeah, but where does it lead?" Boz said, picking a twig from his fur.

"Hopefully, somewhere the squirrels can't find us," I said.

Mina shook her head. "I knew those squirrels were trouble."

"What? I was the one – " My mouth snapped shut as my paws began to tickle. Crouching down, I put my cheek to the ground, letting my whiskers touch the earth. There was a faint vibration. The soil underneath seemed to shiver, a stuttered rhythm, as if the roots were trying to speak. "Do you feel that?" I asked.

"Feel what?" asked Mina.

Boz got down low with me. There it was again. *Boom, boom-boom.*

"Humans can't feel things like this. They lack proper equipment." He pointed to his whiskers.

"I know what that is – it's *music*." I lifted my head and twisted my ears to listen. The sound was faint but sweet. I recognized the melody, but I couldn't place it, like I'd heard it a long time ago.

Anyone playing music that beautiful couldn't be bad. They might even agree to help us. It was a stretch, but we didn't have any other ideas. Also, we needed to stay in the bush until the squirrels disappeared, so we might as well find out if whoever was playing the music was friendly.

I crept through the tunnel towards the sound.

"Where are you going?" asked Mina.

"This way. Come on." The path wound right, then left. We stopped at a round opening laced with pink roses and peeked through the leaves to see a clearing. In the centre was a plump pigeon reclining on a red velvet cushion.

This was no ordinary pigeon. I could tell that right away. A ruby-and-gold tiara sparkled on her head, and a necklace made of tiny gold coins cascaded down her neck into a *V* shape. Her plumage was pale pink, like the clouds at sunrise, and when she moved, her feathers shimmered with rainbows. It had never occurred to me that pigeons could be pretty, but this one most definitely was. The pigeon cast a royal glance around her rosebush courtyard.

Six more pigeons lounged on blue silk carpets surrounded by fancy silver platters overflowing with dried apricots and hazelnuts. A few of them splashed in a stone fountain as they laughed. Sweet sandalwood incense surrounded them in a haze of aromatic splendour.

My stomach growled as I looked at the platters of food. I couldn't even remember how long it had been since I'd eaten a full meal. One of the pigeons poured a cup of tea for the gold-crowned pigeon, and I raised my nose to sniff. It smelled like apples, the same tea Zehra Hala had made for breakfast.

"What is this place?" I whispered.

"I don't know," said Mina, "but I don't think they'd like us spying on them."

"Why?" I asked.

"Quiet." Boz pointed. "One of them is about to sing."

A brown-speckled songbird, small-boned and slight, bowed in front of the crowned pigeon, then picked up a round drum.

She nodded to two other songbirds sitting nearby. One had a guitar shaped like a teardrop; the other had a wooden flute. The drumming started first, the rhythm slinking forwards, beat by beat, then the flute and guitar followed. The sound of it was so luscious and slow, it reminded me of waking up from a good dream but still being half asleep.

The songbird raised her beak and started to sing a round high note. She held it there, letting it rise even higher into the sky, until she sent it plunging downwards as if the sound were tumbling over a waterfall. The vibrations in her voice slowed on the low note, becoming a broad river of sweet and sad. The emotion of it was so real I could almost taste the song, like honey mixed with tears. The bird twirled as she sang, her wings spread, her feathers trembling, all the while keeping time with her drum. The music pulled me close and spiralled around me as I listened to the words:

Cloud over cloud in the sky,
Clouds with darkness,
Clouds with rain.
How many mountains will I pass?
I want to be home,
I want to be home.

I closed my eyes and my mind travelled. I knew this song – I'd heard it before. Baba had sung it to me.

He used to sing to me in Turkish when I was little, usually just before bed. He hadn't done it in a long time – not since he'd got so busy at work – but I remembered it, all the same.

The last time he'd sung it to me, I must've been five years old, or maybe six. We were sitting on the back porch drinking pink lemonade. It was getting dark and the fireflies were coming out, doing their low-rising dances in the back garden. Baba brought out his guitar and began singing to me. It was the same song the bird was singing in the rosebush, but his voice was rumbling and slow. He had the sound of someone who had lost something important, but I hadn't been able to understand what the words meant. After it was over, his face broke into a wide smile like the sun after a storm and his love warmed me.

Somehow, I'd forgotten that memory. Maybe I hadn't wanted to remember. It was easier to pretend I didn't care than to admit how much I had missed spending time with him.

I wondered if he still remembered the song. Of all the things I could've wished at that moment, I wished I could've shared that melody with him. Maybe he could sing to me when I got back.

If I found a way back.

The tune ended. The song echoed inside me like delicate thunder . . . until I got a sharp tug on my tail.

"What was that for?" I demanded.

"They're going to see you!" Mina pointed at my tail, which was glowing again. The rosebush tunnel flickered with my tail's glittering light.

Boz jumped backwards and squeaked. "What kind of cat *are* you?"

"*Shh*," whispered Mina. "They'll hear us."

Boz was nearly hyperventilating. "But her tail sparkles!"

"You have to hide me. Quick!" I said to Mina.

That's when I felt cold steel against my ribs.

10
THE NUTTY ESCAPE

A giant seagull loomed over me, its glare so hot I could feel it in the back of my skull. He snarled at me as he dug his sword into my side, and my legs suddenly felt loose, like they'd lost their bones. Out of the corner of my eye, I could see Boz and Mina. One seagull had a sword at Mina's throat. Another had a sharp talon wrapped around Boz's tail.

They shoved us forwards into the clearing as the music halted.

Chattering shrieks suddenly split the air with a puff of fluttering feathers.

"Intruders!" squawked one of the pigeons.

"Trespassers!"

"Prowlers!"

"QUIET," bellowed the gold-crowned pigeon. There was a sudden silence among the pigeons.

The crowned pigeon got to her feet, scowling at us over her beak. I didn't know birds could scowl, but this one could. She strutted forwards silently, her eyes digging into mine.

"No one enters my court without my permission." Her tone was low and sharp, strung tight with fury.

I swallowed hard. I had to say something, but what? My voice drained to a frightened whisper. "Please let us go," I croaked.

The crowned pigeon leaned down and stared at me like I was a puzzle. A look passed over her face like she'd worked something out, and she leaned back. "Guards, let them go," she said.

I was surprised. That wasn't what I thought she was going to do, but I was happy to be free. Boz scrambled to my side. I pressed against Mina, and the three of us held still.

The seagulls dropped their swords and took their places next to the crowned pigeon.

The crowned pigeon beckoned to me. I raised my eye whiskers like a question. *Me?* She nodded. My legs were still trembling, but there was nothing else I could do. Taking a deep breath, I stepped forwards.

"My name is Gaga," said the crowned one. "I am the ruler here. This area is strictly forbidden to trespassers."

She wore a crown full of rubies and called herself a ruler, so I guessed I was supposed to curtsy, but I wasn't sure how to do it with four paws. If I bent my hind legs, it'd look like I was squatting in a litter tray. I was pretty sure she'd find that insulting, so instead I bent my front legs and bowed my head as low as I could. Hopefully I wasn't doing it wrong. If I made a mistake, she didn't seem like the type who would understand.

I decided to make my tone as formal as possible, like the old medieval fairy tales I'd read. "We are sorry, My Lady. My friends and I are lost. We seek your aid." That sounded old-fashioned, didn't it?

Gaga bowed her head to me. I guess I'd done it right. "I will accept your apology, but you must still leave." She tilted her head at me. "You are not a normal cat, are you? There is something odd about you, I can feel it. Magic has touched you."

She was right, of course, but how could she tell?

"Your tail," she said, as if reading my mind. She must've seen it shimmering.

"Yes, My Lady," I admitted.

"Magic?" Boz hopped around excitedly. "*Real* magic? That's why your tail glowed?"

A twitter went up among the pigeons.

"Calm down, Boz," I said. "You're upsetting them."

"But it's amazing!" he exclaimed.

"I don't understand. Did you do this to her, Mister Rat?" asked Gaga.

"Me? No." He shook his head. "I can't even perform simple tricks, let alone real magic."

"Then who did?" she asked.

"That's why we need your help. We're looking for Mustafa the Great," I said.

A sudden chaos of screeches sounded at the mention of his name.

Gaga's face turned stone hard. "QUIET!" she shouted once again. "Guards, take them away immediately."

The seagulls grabbed us and shoved us towards the exit.

"Wait. I don't understand," I said. "We're looking for a man."

"Mustafa the Great is no man. He is a *jinn* – and he's not just any jinn. He is a treacherous one."

I blinked, trying to understand. "What's a jinn?"

"Perhaps you've heard them called genies. Do you not know these magical creatures?"

My mind reeled as I struggled for words, but all I could get out was a whispered "Oh." I didn't know much about genies apart from what I'd read in books, but I thought they were supposed to pop out of a lamp and grant three wishes. Whoever found the genie controlled them and got whatever they wanted. I hadn't got what I wanted, that was for sure, and the riddle had said it would grant one wish, not three. Plus, my wish hadn't come true. It seemed the books I'd read were wrong about how genies worked, which meant I knew exactly *nothing* about Mustafa the Great.

I sank to the floor. "But . . . the riddle said he would grant my wish and he didn't."

"You thought a jinn would obey your commands, did you?" Gaga clucked at me. "I will tell you a story. A young mother once brought her son to see Mustafa. This mother only wanted the best for her child, so she asked him to make her son happy. Mustafa kindly agreed to fulfil her wish. After a flash of light, the mother discovered Mustafa had turned her son into a donkey. When she complained, he replied: 'Donkeys are always happy', which meant her son would always be happy," she said. "Only the foolish believe they can control jinns with wishes. They are treacherous supernatural creatures who do whatever they please, and if they fulfil wishes, they do so as they see fit."

Gaga was right. I'd asked to go home, and the jinn had fulfilled my wish by turning me into a cat. If I'd known how dangerous jinns were, I never would have rubbed the magic ink bottle.

The seagull jabbed the tip of his sword into my ribs.

I yelped. "Please! We need your help." The squirrels from the Grand Bazaar had to be waiting outside.

Gaga shook her head. "I am sorry. You have been touched by the magic of Mustafa the Great, which means he is bound to you in some way, though you may not yet understand exactly how. I will not have this jinn or his perilous magic anywhere near me."

With a final thrust, the seagull heaved me out through a small opening in the hedge wall.

I blinked in the light. Before I could get a look around, someone yanked my whiskers. I turned to see Boz and Mina crouched behind a statue of a lion. Boz waved me over, then pointed across the path to a back gate.

"There they are," he whispered.

The squirrels guarded the exit, watching the area for movement. My heartbeat knocked in my ears.

"Why are they still following us?" Mina asked.

"They're stubborn." Boz shook his head. "My uncle Beyaz found a songbird with a broken wing, and he liked her so much he built a little house with a feeder for her. But then a squirrel worked out there was free food and wouldn't leave the bird feeder alone. Uncle Beyaz did everything he could to keep the squirrel away, but that little beast never gave up."

"What happened?" I asked.

"One day, the bird's wing healed," he said.

"So she flew away?"

"No, she punched the squirrel. Right in the snout. He was so surprised, he ran away and never came back." Boz smiled widely at me. "A small but mighty bird."

I eyed the big squirrel, remembering the feel of his razor-sharp teeth on my neck. He didn't look like the type to get surprised and run away. There was no way I was mighty enough to take him on.

"We can't go back into the hedge. What are we going to do?" Mina asked.

I scoured my brain for ideas. "I don't know."

"We can't stay. They'll work out we're here eventually. Squirrels are extremely clever," said Boz.

A hazelnut slid out from under Boz's coat and plunked to the ground. He quickly scooped it up and stuffed it into his pocket.

"Is that a hazelnut? Did you steal it from Gaga?" I asked.

"I only took one," he said defensively. Three more nuts fell out of his coat. "Or four."

Mina and I stared in surprise.

"Don't look at me like that. Rats are natural thieves. It's instinct." He sniffed.

Instinct. I remembered the trick the shop owner had used on the squirrel, and it gave me an idea – one that just might work. "Mina, I need you to throw those nuts over by the gate."

"You're going to give the squirrels a treat?" asked Boz.

"Just do it," I said.

"All right. I'll try." Mina peeked around the side of the statue. She tossed the nuts and then ducked back, unseen.

The big squirrel's eyes popped when he saw the nuts. He made a loud chirp and the other squirrels turned to look too.

"What's supposed to happen?" asked Mina.

"*Shh*. Wait." I watched intently, hoping my plan would work.

The big squirrel took one last look around, then dived to the ground and grabbed a nut, just like he had in the shop. The squirrel jumped up, leapt over the wall and disappeared. Then the other squirrels did the same, until one by one they all disappeared.

It *worked*. I'd managed to get rid of them.

I grinned proudly. "Natural animal instinct."

"Very clever," said Boz, "except for the part where now I don't have any snacks."

"We're safe. Come on, let's go," I said.

We poked our heads out from behind the statue, then scurried across the cobblestone path. Mina opened the gate door, and the three of us escaped.

11
THE DOG WHO COULD EAT LIONS

Mina darted across a crowded street. Eight horses and carts lined up, waiting for passengers. She ducked down next to one of them. Boz and I were both tucked inside her waistcoat. Boz fitted easily, but I didn't. I poked my head out. Grey clouds lined the sky as raindrops began to drizzle down. A chill shook my shoulders. I burrowed my nose into Mina's jacket to talk to Boz.

"Boz, you said you knew where Mustafa was. Which way should we go?" I asked.

He rubbed his nose. "Actually, I said I *might* know."

"What does that mean? Do you know where he is, or don't you?" I kept my voice steady.

He wrung his paws sheepishly. "I don't. I'm sorry."

"But – but you said . . ."

I couldn't believe it. Boz had *lied* to me. The warmth drained from my cheeks. If Boz didn't know where Mustafa the Great was, then I was back at square one. I had no clues and no hope of getting home.

Mina nudged me. I poked my head out again as she pointed

to a cart. "I've seen that driver over there before. He drops off goods at my house sometimes. I overheard him saying he was headed to my neighbourhood now."

"Why do you want to go home? Aunt Sibel was furious when you left. She'll be waiting there to punish you," I said.

"Then I have to take my punishment. Hopefully, it's not too bad." Her forehead wrinkled nervously, then she shook it off. "We need to get out of the rain, find some food and think things over. I'll hide you in the attic and we can start fresh tomorrow."

"We can't give up. I have to find Mustafa!" I said, pushing my way out of Mina's jacket to jump to the ground. My paws splashed down in mud.

"You heard what Gaga said. Mustafa is a dangerous jinn. He could do anything he wants to you," she said.

She was right. There was no way to know if he'd be willing to undo whatever spell he'd put on me. I shook off the thought. "He's the only creature who can turn me back into a girl. I have to try. We *can't* give up."

"Nobody is giving up," said Mina. "I said I'd help you and I will, but there's nothing more we can do tonight. It's getting dark."

Boz poked his head out of Mina's jacket. "Those squirrels could still be looking for us too."

"I agree. We should get indoors," said Mina.

Part of me knew they were right, but everything was happening too fast – I couldn't think.

Mina picked me up and held me under her arm. "Here

comes the driver. Quick, get onto the cart."

A potbellied man with a thickly stubbled chin heaved himself into the driver's seat and grabbed his whip. Mina pushed me under a tarp and jumped into the cart as it jolted forwards.

The cart squeaked down the cobblestone street. Raindrops pitter-pattered on the tarp above us. Boz slid out of Mina's jacket and huddled down next to her.

I glared at him as I twitched my tail.

"I know what you're thinking," said Boz.

"No, you don't," I said.

He couldn't possibly. My thoughts were moving too fast, chasing each other in circles. Gaga's speech about Mustafa the Great had scared me. The idea of facing him made me dizzy with fear. What if he made things worse? It was hard to imagine anything worse than being a cat lost in a time warp, but every time I thought things couldn't get worse, they did.

"This probably isn't the best time to ask for a favour, but I'd like to tag along on your search," said Boz.

I intensified my glare. "Why did you lie to me?"

"It wasn't a lie, exactly," said Boz.

I blinked angrily at him. "It wasn't the truth either."

He sighed. "I'm sorry, Dalya, I truly am. But I was hungry and –"

I stomped a paw. It did not feel good. "You got my hopes up. I thought you knew him."

"I know, and I want to make it up to you. Hear me out: I helped you get away from those squirrels at the Grand Bazaar, right? And I stole those nuts, which we used at the rosebush. Plus, rats are naturally clever. I could be useful to you."

This was possibly true. "Why do you want to come with us? Tell the whole truth this time."

"I want to meet Mustafa the Great. How many chances does anyone get to see *real* magic?"

"You want something from him, don't you?"

He paused, as if embarrassed by his answer. "Yes," he admitted. "I'm hoping to ask him to turn me into a successful magician."

"He might turn you into a frog."

"Maybe that wouldn't be a bad thing." He rubbed his nose. "I've heard the Frog Bazaar is nice. Good prices too. Some of the frogs even get kissed."

I eyed him sideways to see if he was serious. He smiled and shook his head. "I'm only joking. But," he said, "the truth is, I'm tired of being a failure. If I go with you, there's a chance he *might* grant my wish. I'm willing to take the risk."

I pursed my lips and considered his request. Boz was right that he hadn't exactly lied to me, and he had said he was sorry. He had turned out to be extremely helpful when he stole those nuts from Gaga. Plus, I had no leads on Mustafa's location, and I didn't have many friends. The more eyes searching for him, the better.

I nodded to Boz as the cart slowed.

Mina peered out from underneath the tarp. "This is it."

The driver pulled to a stop in front of Mina's house and got off the cart to secure the horse. As soon as he was out of sight, Mina gestured for us to follow. Boz and I slid out after her.

Rain bucketed down. As we stepped into the deluge, my fur matted instantly, and my whiskers drooped. Taking the long way around so we wouldn't get spotted, we dashed across the mud-splattered courtyard to hide behind a tree before we made our way towards Mina's house. Clouds dimmed the twilight sky, and the faint smell of a smoky fireplace wafted from a nearby chimney. We crept from one tree to the next until we came to the back door.

Boz shook the raindrops from his whiskers. "So, what's the plan? I hope it involves food."

"It does. But first, we have to get inside the house. The doors are locked and Aunt Sibel keeps the keys around her neck," said Mina.

A flash of lightning lit up the courtyard as the back door swung open. Aunt Sibel stood in a rectangle of light. The driver of our cart carried out a wooden shipping crate and loaded it onto the back of the cart.

We crouched behind a tree to hide, then nosed around the trunk to watch Aunt Sibel.

"Those are the crates I saw in the broom cupboard," I whispered.

"Really?" Mina craned her head, trying to get a look. "Come on, let's find out what she's doing."

"Don't you think we should stay here? What if she sees me?" I asked.

"This is my chance to see what she's been hiding in the broom cupboard. I have to find out if she's been lying to me about my father," said Mina.

I could understand why she wanted to know. "We have to be careful." If Aunt Sibel caught me, there was no telling what she'd do. But it definitely wouldn't be good.

Mina nodded. "Let's go."

We moved closer, sneaking from bush to bush, until we could hear what they were saying.

"There are twelve children's silk dresses in the crate. Make sure Ali Bey pays for every single one of them. I want my money's worth," said Aunt Sibel.

"Of course, Lady Sibel," said the driver.

"They're the finest dresses Bursa has to offer. My brother wouldn't send anything less than the best. I want a good price. If I hear Ali Bey is cheating me, I will be angry." Aunt Sibel wagged her finger at the driver. "Remember what I did to Hasan Bey."

The driver paled. "Yes, Lady Sibel, I remember."

"Good. I want the gold here by morning," said Aunt Sibel. "I have things to buy for tomorrow's party."

The driver bowed to her, then climbed onto the cart and cracked his whip. As the horse trotted forwards, Aunt Sibel glanced around the courtyard before she closed the back door and locked it.

Mina's mouth hung open and her cheeks turned red. "My father has been sending me silk dresses. He's been sending me things all along, and Aunt Sibel lied about it. She's been selling them and using the gold to pay for her parties."

"I'm so sorry, Mina." I didn't know what else to do, so I crawled into her lap and leaned into her chest.

She wrapped her arms around me. We were both soaked to the bone with rain, but it didn't matter. Her hug felt nice.

She knuckled a tear from her chin. "I thought he didn't care about me."

I nodded. "She probably wanted you to think that."

Mina swiped her nose with her sleeve. "Last year she made me write him a letter saying how happy I was living with her. She made me say she was treating me well. No one loves an ungrateful child, she said. If I were grateful, maybe my father would love me. But she was lying to me the whole time."

"It sounds like she lied to your dad too," I said.

Mina blinked at me. "You're right. I didn't even think about that."

If Mina's dad did love her, then he would want to know what Aunt Sibel was doing to Mina. "Do you know where your dad is? Could you write him another letter?"

"This time of year, he's always trading in Bursa." Mina shook her head. "What if he doesn't believe me? What if Aunt Sibel finds out about the letter?"

Mina was right – it would be risky to write to her father, but if she didn't try, nothing would change. Aunt Sibel would keep stealing, and Mina would keep living in that house with her. At least Mina knew now that her dad cared about her. That was one good thing.

"Thank you for being my friend." She hugged me tight. "If it weren't for you, I never would've found out about this."

I leaned my head on her shoulder. "I'm glad to be – "

My voice halted as a familiar smell wafted past my nose.

I turned to see two copper-coloured eyes. Out of the shadows crept a dog as large as a lion. It had cream-coloured fur, and its ears were tipped with brown.

The same dog I'd seen from the open window my first night here – I was sure of it.

Its black mouth salivated around a long row of jagged teeth. He opened his massive jaws and a rumbling growl vibrated in his throat. My whole body could fit into his mouth.

The three of us gasped in unison as we pressed together and backed away.

"What is it with you two?" squeaked Boz. "If you're not getting chased by squirrels, it's *this* monster."

Mina's voice quivered. "What are we going to do?"

"I vote we don't get eaten," said Boz.

"Agreed," said Mina.

We'd never be able to fight off a dog that size. If we wanted to survive, we didn't have a lot of choices. *"Run!"* I shouted.

We whirled around and sprinted past bushes towards the cobblestone street. The rain came down in sheets now, making it hard to see. Mina desperately whipped her head back and forth, then pointed. "This way!"

We darted into an alley between two houses. The dog followed, his claws scratching the street as he chased us. Stinging pain ripped through my body as I tried to turn the tight corner and instead smacked into a stone wall. Mina and Boz screeched to a halt. We whirled to face the giant dog. He had us cornered.

Boz scaled the wall and called from the top. "Come on!"

But the wall was too high for me. Mina clambered halfway up and fell.

The dog stalked forwards, his fiery eyes narrowed on us as he inched closer. A wave of electric fear shot down to my spine as I opened my mouth to shriek, but nothing came out.

Mina's face hardened like she'd made a decision. She vaulted in front of me, blocking the dog's way. "You leave us alone!" Her whole body trembled but she held her fists up, ready to fight.

"Mina, don't!" I shouted.

"I'm tired of being scared all the time." Mina steadied her breath. "I won't let you hurt my friends!"

The dog stopped in his tracks. We held still, waiting to see what the dog would do next, but he didn't move. He didn't bark or growl. He watched us for a moment, then let out a soft whine as he lay down on the ground and put his nose between his paws.

Mina lowered her shaking fists.

Boz let out a laugh. "The dog is scared of *you*. Hah!" he crowed. "That's hilarious!"

Mina looked at the dog carefully. "No, he isn't scared of me." She stepped forwards slightly and offered the dog a formal bow. The dog stood up and bowed back.

"You're not here to hurt us. Are you?" asked Mina.

The dog shook his head no.

She reached out to pet the dog. He tilted his head and let out a whimpering sigh as she scratched behind his ears. "You don't say much, do you?"

The dog shook his head again.

"My name is Mina," she said. "These are my friends Dalya and Boz. Dalya looks like a cat, but she's actually a girl. We're trying to find a jinn called Mustafa the Great who did this to her."

The dog pricked up his ears.

"What is it? Do you know him?" she asked.

"You're asking the dog if he knows a jinn?" Boz snorted.

"He might. You never know until you ask," Mina shot back.

The dog sprang to his feet and gestured with his head like he wanted us to follow him. He took several steps, then turned around and made the same gesture again.

"See? He wants us to come with him," said Mina.

"You can help us find Mustafa the Great?" I asked.

The dog nodded.

"Are you kidding me? We're going to follow a dog?" Boz asked.

"Do you have any better ideas?" asked Mina.

"Yes, I do. We turn around and leave," snapped Boz. "Remember I told you rats were clever animals? Well, I'm very clever, and I'm telling you: I heard his stomach grumbling."

"He's not going to eat us," said Mina.

"Oh, really? I suppose you've got a lot of experience living on the streets with animals."

"Well, no, but – "

"You can't trust a dog that big! They're hungry all the time. That's how they get so big. He might seem nice now, but at some point, he's going to change his mind and have me as a snack," said Boz. "Dalya too."

I studied the dog. I wasn't sure I should trust him. When I'd met Boz, he'd told me he knew where Mustafa was, and he'd been lying. What if this dog was lying too?

But I didn't have a choice. I had no clues and no idea how to find Mustafa. Could I really afford to walk away from an offer of help? If there was any chance this dog was telling the truth, I needed to follow him – no matter how dangerous it might be.

I'd made up my mind. "I say we go with him." My voice was firm.

"I agree. There's no sense standing out here in the rain all night," said Mina.

Boz flicked his glance between us. "You're serious?"

I nodded.

Boz let out an irritated sigh. "Fine. I'll go. But if we get eaten, I'm blaming you."

12

THE UNEXPECTED PHILOSOPHER

The rain drizzled to a stop and the clouds cleared from the sky. Boz, Mina and I trailed single file behind the dog down a hill strewn with weeds. It was dark now, but the *C*-shaped moon and a single star were reflected in the puddles that dotted the dirt path, lighting our way. Somewhere around the footbridge, Boz decided he'd had enough walking and asked Mina to carry him in her pocket. Every once in a while, he'd get startled and squeak.

As we neared the bottom of the hill, I knew we were getting close to the sea. I could taste it in the air, though I couldn't see it because it was blocked by a brick wall taller than the trees. The dog muscled his way up a steep stairway that cut diagonally along the side of the wall. He stopped when he got to the top, where there was a pointy-capped castle tower with two hollow windows that looked like a stone soldier's empty eyes. I darted up after him, climbing the stairs easily with my springy hind legs.

The dog waited patiently for Mina to catch up with us at

the top of the stairs, then he nosed through a heavy wooden door. Inside was a single room with a packed-dirt floor and a ringed firepit in the centre. Under the window, a sliver of moonlight lit a potted red tulip.

Boz hopped out of Mina's pocket and looked around. "Is this it? We hiked twenty minutes for this?"

I poked Boz in the ribs with my tail. "Don't be rude."

The room was bare, but it smelled like freshly baked bread. My belly gurgled.

"You are hungry." A deep voice rumbled with old age. I rotated my ears, straining to work out where it was coming from, but every sound in the tower room echoed.

"Who said that?" I asked.

"Wasn't me," said Boz.

"How about you?" I looked at the dog suspiciously.

The dog shook his head.

"Come, sit by me," said the voice.

I twisted around again, anxiously scanning the room as I coiled my muscles, ready for anything.

"I don't know where you are," I said.

"Here," said the voice.

I turned towards the sound, frowning when I spied the potted flower. On the lip of the tulip was a curly brown shell and two outstretched tentacle eyes that were black and tiny. I relaxed. *It's a snail.*

Inching closer, I leaned down. It seemed to me the snail's eyes looked both old and wise, though I couldn't have explained why.

"My name is Salyangoz," said the snail.

I nodded a greeting. "I'm Dalya."

"Come. Sit. Azman will get you some food," he said.

"Azman?" I asked. "You mean the dog? He doesn't say much."

Salyangoz slowly shook his head. "Azman is shy. He always has been, ever since I met him."

I kept my eyes on the dog. "I saw him the first night I was here."

"He came to warn you about the squirrels. The same group kidnapped him when he was a puppy. I believe he's worried you will be kidnapped too. Like Azman, you are a special breed. He is not just any dog. He is an Anatolian shepherd. And you are not just any cat. You are a Turkish Angora, but it's your odd-coloured eyes that make you truly valuable."

"So he was trying to help me all along?" I'd been so caught up in my own situation, I hadn't stopped to consider the possibility that he was trying to be nice. "Thank you."

Azman whined softly and nodded in response, then dipped his head shyly.

Mina and Boz had already taken a seat around the warm fire. I joined them, toasting one side of my body, then the other, and my fur began to dry, starting with my tail. Azman busied himself on the other side of the room. Whatever he was doing, it smelled delicious.

"Now that you are settled, tell me why you are here. Azman never brings anyone here unless they are in dire need of a philosopher," said Salyangoz.

I cocked my head at him, trying to think of any problem I'd ever had that required a philosopher. "Actually, I need a jinn."

"Why?" Salyangoz sounded surprised.

I explained as quickly as I could what had happened with the ink bottle and the riddle. When I stopped talking, Salyangoz nodded thoughtfully.

"That *is* a problem that only Mustafa the Great can solve," he agreed. "But Azman was right to bring you here. You are in luck, my dear, because I happen to know how you can find him."

My heart rattled against my ribs. "Are you serious?"

"Go to the court of the Cat Sultan. It's on the second level of the red brick minaret next to the Hagia Sophia. Azman will lead you there," he said. "The Cat Sultan is friends with Mustafa the Great. He can set up a meeting between you two."

"So, the Cat Sultan will help me find him?" I ventured. "I'll be able see Mustafa the Great?"

"Yes, my dear, you heard correctly," he said.

"That's wonderful!" exclaimed Mina.

"See, everything worked out," said Boz.

I couldn't believe how easy that had been. It was almost too good to be true – but Salyangoz had said he was sure the Cat Sultan could help us, and I let myself believe it. Joy bounced inside me as I hopped onto Mina's shoulder and down into her lap. Giggling, she squished me in a hug. Boz danced around in excitement.

Salyangoz laughed as he watched us celebrate. "It's not

every day I make my guests so happy! Azman, how about some food and drink for our guests?"

"Did someone say *food*?" Boz dug out a cloth napkin from his pocket and tucked it under his neck like a bib, then grinned as Mina and I laughed. "What? I always come prepared for snacks."

Salyangoz laughed too.

The room filled with scrumptious smells as Azman placed dish after dish filled with warm buttered rice, thinly sliced spiced meat, sweet-and-salty green beans, and crunchy toast in front of us. Boz heaped his plate, and Mina nibbled on the beans. I tried to enjoy every bite, but I was so hungry I swallowed huge mouthfuls of rice without really tasting it. We ate and ate, and Azman refilled our plates again and again, until we were so full, we could hardly move.

"You aren't finished yet, my friends!" said Salyangoz. "I say we break out the sherbet!"

"Sherbet?" I asked.

"It's a tasty drink, like a special dessert," said Salyangoz. Azman hopped to his feet and offered us each a small cup of pink liquid.

I sniffed it. "It smells like . . . roses."

"Yes," said Salyangoz. "We boil rose petals and add sugar, then let it cool. There is nothing better."

I leaned forwards and tasted it. Floral sweetness blossomed on my tongue, like a candied garden, and I lapped up every drop. Mina drank hers slowly, savouring every bit, and Boz asked for two more servings.

Boz licked his lips and got to his feet. "How about a little music?"

"Oh yes!" said Mina.

Boz pulled two tiny wooden spoons the size of toothpicks from his jacket. He tucked them between two fingers in his paw, then used his thumb to clack them together. He knocked out a rhythm – *one-two, one-two, one-two-three* – as he began to dance, skipping from side to side. He grinned, his belly jiggling. Mina leapt to her feet and joined him, snapping her fingers in time to his beat, and then Azman got up too.

"Come on, Dalya. Dance with us!" called Mina.

Embarrassed, I shook my head no. "I don't know how to dance."

"I'll help you!" she said.

Before I could say no, Mina pulled me into her arms and began to dance with me. At first I was scared she would drop me, so I dug my claws into her waistcoat, but as we turned and turned, a wild glee rocked my body and a laugh erupted from my lungs. I couldn't help it. The room spun with happiness, and the music matched my galloping heartbeat. Boz let out a whoop of delight as we joined him, all of us prancing in a circle, and he sang:

Sometimes like the wind, I whirl
Sometimes like the dust, I drift
One day we will forget these troubles
So let's dance and sing today!

We twirled together in time with the music. Then his rhythm began to change, getting faster and faster, until we were practically running and spinning all at the same time. Mina held on to me tightly as Boz rattled out a loud finale and we collapsed onto each other in a heap of giggles.

"That was marvellous!" said Salyangoz.

It was, it really was. As the laughter slowed, we caught our breath. Mina offered a hug to Azman and I turned to Boz.

"You play wonderful music," I said.

"Thank you." He stood up and gave an elaborate bow, then tucked his spoons back into his jacket pocket.

"Why didn't you decide to become a musician?" I asked.

"You mean, why do I keep trying to be a magician even though I'm not good at it?" he asked.

I didn't want to say yes, but that was what I had been thinking. "No," I lied.

"It's okay. I've wondered that myself sometimes. I've always wanted to be a magician, ever since I can remember. That's my dream. I've just got to practise and work at it. My grandmother used to say to me: 'Don't give up. It's usually the last key on the ring that opens the door.'"

"That sounds like good advice," I said.

He nodded. "Well, she was locked in a cabinet when she said it. But that doesn't mean it isn't good advice."

"Oh?" I wasn't sure if I was supposed to laugh or not.

He chuckled like he'd enjoyed watching my surprise. "Don't worry, we got her out. She was a lovely lady, but she did forget where she was going from time to time when she got older, which got her into trouble."

Mina poked the fire, which had already begun to die down to embers, then patted me gently on the back. "We should get some rest," she said.

I nodded to her. Our plans were set for the next day. We would leave early in the morning, set out for the court of the Cat Sultan, and find Mustafa the Great. My belly was stuffed, and my legs were tired. Mina wrapped her arm around me, and Boz snuggled into my side, all of us warm by the fire. I allowed myself to be happy for a moment. Before long, I was fast asleep.

I didn't stay asleep long. Everyone else was happily snoozing as they nestled together, but the late-night quiet seemed to make my thoughts louder, and all my doubts crowded into my mind, all speaking at once. Would I be able to find Mustafa? Would he help me?

I shifted restlessly, curling up this way and that, until finally I gave up. I nudged the tower door open, slipped outside and leapt up to the side of the wall.

I had a perfect view of the sea. Chilly salt air ruffled my fur at the neck. Below, two fishing boats and a three-sailed ship slid across the water. I crouched down and watched the reflected moonlight split in their wake.

I was worried about meeting Mustafa, that was for sure, but there was something else bothering me too. If everything went right tomorrow, and Mustafa agreed to turn me back into a girl, then I'd see Baba again. My problems would be solved, but Mina's wouldn't. She'd still have to deal with Aunt Sibel, and she'd have to do it by herself. It wasn't fair to Mina, especially since I was the reason she'd left the house and got into trouble in the first place.

"Your necklace is pretty," said Salyangoz.

"Oh!" I jumped, surprised. The snail must've followed me outside, but it had clearly taken him a while to catch up. "My necklace?"

He turned his tentacle eyes to my neck, and I glanced down. I'd forgotten the necklace Zehra Hala had given me.

I watched the snail, thinking, as my whiskers twitched. There was something I wanted to ask. It was an odd question, one that might be fit for a philosopher.

"On my sixth birthday, Baba took me to the river park for a picnic. After I made my wish on a cupcake, he kissed the top of my head and said the word mashallah." I'd meant to ask about the word. That picnic was the day before he told me he was moving out, and after that, it didn't seem to matter. Now I wished I'd asked. "Zehra Hala said the same word when she gave me this necklace. Can you tell me what it means?"

"Mashallah has many special meanings," he said. "Usually, you say it when you notice something wonderful or beautiful about someone you love. It's a way of asking for protection. That good-luck charm necklace is also meant to protect you."

"From what?"

"Jealousy, envy. We call it the Evil Eye," he said. "Saying

mashallah reminds us that everything good in this world is exactly as God willed it. You say it when you feel thankful for the goodness your loved ones have been given and you want to keep them safe from anyone who would take it away, but it only works if you say it with your whole heart."

I turned the word over in my head, saying it again and again. Mashallah was a marvellous word. How could something so small say so much? How could it make me feel so many things at once?

My chest tightened. I couldn't even guess how long I'd been gone, but Baba had to be searching for me. Right before I'd rubbed the bottle, he'd panicked when he couldn't find me for fifteen minutes.

This wasn't the only time I'd disappeared on Baba. Right before he moved out, my mum had gone away for a conference. He was packing up his things upstairs, but I didn't want him to leave, so I built a den down in the basement and stayed there all day. I'd just gone upstairs to grab another box of crackers when I saw the blue-and-red lights outside our house. Baba was standing on the front lawn, surrounded by policemen with torches. His chest moved up and down in jagged heaves like he was upset.

I hadn't realized he'd been looking for me. I'd thought he probably wouldn't care since he was planning to leave, anyway. When I stepped outside and called his name, he didn't yell at me. He hugged me so tightly that I could hardly breathe. I remember how his arms trembled.

After the divorce, I'd been angry with Baba, and I'd assumed he worked all the time because he didn't care about me, but maybe that wasn't true. Maybe he had always cared about me. Maybe I'd been unfair to him.

All of this was so confusing. I crouched down, making my body as small as possible. "I feel so lost."

"Everyone feels lost," said Salyangoz. "The difference is, most people don't do anything about it. But you are searching for answers. That means you are bound to find out something true and real about who you are."

I slanted my eyes at him. I couldn't think of anything I'd learned about myself by becoming a cat. The only thing I'd discovered was that I could land on four feet in an emergency.

"You don't believe me, do you?" he said.

I shrugged.

"Give it time," he said. "Sometimes the things we seek are also seeking us."

I nodded at him, but I wasn't sure I understood. I turned my face back to the water. A sound lifted in the breeze, a round note vibrating with sacred intensity. The sound was majestic. I looked around, trying to work out where it was coming from. From the top of the wall, where I sat, I could see a man standing on a high balcony of a spiky minaret tower, his arms open as he lifted his face up to call out. His reverent melody took flight, rising and twirling in the sky.

"You are in luck, my dear," said Salyangoz.

"Why is that?" I asked.

He pointed his tentacle eyes towards the bay. "Because this the perfect place to watch the cranes do their dance."

Five white cranes with long necks flew towards the moonlight. Every move they made was graceful, and every beat of their wings was done in perfect unison.

The cranes slowed to a stop, floating in the air for a moment. One by one, they pointed their beaks towards heaven, then each one began to spin. Around and around they whirled, their white wings stretched wide.

I sat perfectly still, spellbound by their magnificence as they spun in perfect, slow circles, until the singing ended. I didn't even need to look down to know the tip of my tail was glowing again. I could feel it. The warmth spread upwards along the ridge of my back until it wrapped around me like a blanket.

Salyangoz smiled at me. "On a night when the wind is perfect, the sail just needs to be open and the world is full of beauty. Tonight is such a night," he said. "Come, my child. You must sleep. You've got a big day tomorrow."

I took one last look at the glittering water before I followed Salyangoz back inside, curled up next to Mina and went back to sleep.

13

THE COURT OF THE CAT SULTAN

I saw Baba clearly. He stood at the top of Zehra Hala's staircase, every muscle in his body tensed, blood vessels climbing his neck like vines, his mouth gaping open in a shout. He was calling my name.

I was at the bottom of the stairs, but for some reason he couldn't see me. I called to him again, saying *I'm here*, but he couldn't hear me. I screamed –

"*Dalya.*" Mina shook me gently. "You were having a bad dream."

I stared up at her, dazed, my pulse pounding in my ears as I teetered to my feet.

"What was it about?" Mina asked.

I shook my head, trying to remember where I was. "My dad," I said. "What – what are you doing?"

She sat on the floor, holding paper and a feather pen. Her hands were stained with ink. "I was thinking about my father too. I've decided to write a letter to him and ask him to come home. As soon as he gets here, I'm going to tell him about

Aunt Sibel." Her smile dimmed to a frown. "Aunt Sibel will probably say that I'm lying. He may not believe me, but I have to take the chance and tell him what she's been doing. I hope he doesn't take her side."

I was silent. In my experience, adults always sided with other adults unless there was solid proof, and Mina didn't have any. Aunt Sibel didn't seem like the forgiving type, either, so if she found out Mina accused her of stealing, she'd definitely try to take revenge. The image of Aunt Sibel hurling the teacup surfaced in my mind, and I shivered.

I watched as Mina penned another line. Zehra Hala had said something about me setting things right for the family. I had no idea what that meant, but maybe it had something to do with Aunt Sibel and Mina. This was the time for me to say something. I could at least tell Mina who I really was. I could tell her I'd been to her house. I could tell her I'd seen her painting in the hallway before I chased the cat upstairs and found the ink bottle. I could tell her I wasn't just *any* girl who had been turned into a cat by a jinn – I was her great-great-granddaughter.

"I wanted to tell you . . ." I paused, trying to find the right words.

"Yes?" She looked up at me expectantly.

Mina had finally worked up the courage to ask her father to come home and to tell him about Aunt Sibel. I couldn't ruin it by distracting her. She didn't need to know who I was. She should focus on getting her father back.

I cleared my throat. "When you stood up for us yesterday, that was brave," I said instead.

Mina shrugged. "I only did what I had to."

"That's not true. You could've run, but you didn't. You're a good friend, Mina, a true friend. I mean it," I said.

"Aunt Sibel leaves me alone in my room so much, I almost forgot the sound of my own voice. I'm glad I found it again. I owe that to you." She reached out to stroke me. I rubbed my head against Mina's shoulder, then leaned back and watched her, my eyes slowly blinking as a deep purr rumbled in my throat. Purring tickled in a nice way.

As Mina folded up her letter, she tilted her head at me with a half-smile. "I don't mean to be rude, but you've got some mud on your face. It's right here." She pointed to my left cheek.

"What?"

"There's some on your ears and paws too."

I frowned. I'd slept on a packed-dirt floor, so I wasn't surprised I was muddy. The problem was I had no idea how to get the dirt off. It wasn't as if Salyangoz's castle tower had a hot shower and a mirror.

I'd seen cats cleaning themselves before, but that didn't mean I knew how to do it myself. Still, I didn't want to walk around looking dirty.

Rocking back on my haunches, I picked up my front right paw and gazed at it. I stuck out my tongue and held it there for a moment. The idea of eating dirt was extremely disgusting, but licking was how cats got clean, and I was a cat, at least for now. I gave my dusty paw a lick. And another.

The dirt didn't taste like much. It was a little salty and reminded me of the smell of soil after a spring rain shower. There was even something oddly calming about the rhythm of it. In fact, by the time I got to my ears, I caught myself actually purring again.

While I was cleaning myself, Mina fashioned a cloth into a makeshift turban. She hid her long hair underneath the turban, so she looked like a boy again. Azman and Boz cleaned up, and we were finally ready to leave.

I'd just finished licking my whiskers when Salyangoz called to me. I padded over to his tulip. He turned his tentacle eyes towards me and smiled.

"The Cat Sultan should be able to direct you to Mustafa the Great, but there is something you should know," he said. "The Cat Sultan loves having people fawn over him. He finds it very entertaining. There's nothing he enjoys more than a good show. Azman will do his best to help you."

Azman bowed his head to me. I was nervous about meeting Mustafa the Great, but it made me feel better to know I had friends at my side.

I glanced around the room, letting my gaze linger on every face. I couldn't believe how lucky I'd been to have found Mina, Boz, Azman and Salyangoz. We'd had so much fun the night before, dancing and laughing and drinking sweet sherbet, and now they were all helping me get home.

Everything had gone wrong – my wish had backfired, I was

facing the possibility of spending the rest of my life as a cat, and I was worried I'd never see Baba or my mum again, but I'd got one thing right. If I had to be stuck here, like this, at least I wasn't totally alone. I had friends.

Mina stepped forwards with the letter she'd written to her father. "Are you sure it's no trouble, Salyangoz?"

"Not to worry, Mina. I will make sure the cranes deliver this letter to your father today," said Salyangoz. "The cranes are happy to help."

A flutter of downy-white wings landed on the window ledge. A crane extended its long neck and offered a graceful bow to Mina. She returned the gesture, then held out her father's letter to the bird. It gently grasped it in its beak and bowed once more before it flew away.

"Thank you for everything," I said.

"You are all welcome, my dears," he said.

I waved my paw at the snail and said goodbye.

Azman led us through a network of zigzagging cobblestone streets. The morning air was crisp and cool, but the sun was already beginning to warm the breeze. I trotted behind Azman, trying to keep up with the massive dog. He paused at a junction and waited for a line of carriages to pass.

Across from us was a massive building with a grey dome that looked like a helmet and a skinny minaret tower next to it in the shape of a spear. The walls were heavyset and thick, like wide shoulders, and together with its spear and helmet, the place looked like a stone giant squatting on a hill. But the most amazing thing about it was its colour: blazing orange, the colour of the deepest part of the sunset.

We followed Azman through an iron door big enough for an elephant to go through. I wondered why they'd made the door so large, but I guessed it was to impress visitors like me. Inside was even more incredible. The ceiling soared upwards to a high dome that seemed to float on a circle of twinkling glass diamonds. Rays of sunlight streaked down to the granite floors, giving the place a purplish glow.

The four of us gazed up like frozen statues. The hushed silence of the place felt sacred and pure. It hollowed me out, carved a space inside me, quiet as stars. While I couldn't be certain, I felt deep in my bones that there was nowhere else like this magnificent place.

When I'd arrived in Istanbul with Baba, I hadn't wanted to see the city – I'd just wanted to go back home – but everything I'd seen here was more beautiful than I could've imagined: the moonlight on the water, the whirling cranes, the song of the nightingale, and now this place. If I'd got my wish and left, I would've missed all of this.

"You've never been to the Hagia Sophia before?" asked Boz.

I hadn't realized I'd been staring. "No."

Boz looked up. "I've always loved it here. Most rats don't know this, but the Hagia Sophia is more than a thousand years old. Back in those days, nobody had ever tried building a dome that big or that high before, but they did it so well, it's survived earthquakes, fires and a number of wars. The Hagia Sophia changed the history of architecture. Did you know that?"

I shook my head.

"Every conqueror who has ever come to the city stopped here first. This place is the beating heart of Istanbul, and everyone who passes through can feel it."

I gazed at Boz, caught in my own thoughts. I wondered if Baba liked this place. Maybe if I could convince him to stop working, he'd take me here when I got back. He could tell me about its history, and we could talk about how amazing the place was.

If I got back, I reminded myself.

"You're starting to sound like Salyangoz," I said to Boz.

"Oh, I'm no philosopher. I'm just here for the snacks." Boz shrugged like he didn't care, but I could tell he was blushing under his fur. "You think I sound like a philosopher?"

I nodded and laughed as Mina picked him up and put him in her pocket. "Enough sightseeing. Time to go, Mister Philosopher," she said.

Azman ducked down a side hallway, his nails clicking on the granite floor as he led us to a round room with a staircase that spiralled upwards in one long curlicue. Around and around we climbed, up and up, edging close to the walls, until Azman halted in front of a small window.

It was an unusual-looking window, tucked to the side and curtained with cobwebs. If Azman hadn't pointed his nose at it, I might not have seen it. Boz pushed the cobwebs aside. The window showed the trees below, but they were too green, and the light was wrong. I leaned forwards to get a better look. It wasn't a real window – it was a door painted to *look* like a window – a trick.

With a clunk, the bolt unlocked, and the door swung outwards. The largest crow I'd ever seen emerged and hopped forwards. His feathers were black and as shiny as wet stone, and his eyes were milky white with age.

This wasn't the first time I'd met a bird since I was turned into a cat. In Gaga's rosebush, the pigeons had been scared of me – and with good reason. I'd hardly been able to control my natural instincts. But this crow was different. My natural instinct wasn't to chase or bite him. Something inside me told me to run, even though I knew I couldn't. If I wanted to find Mustafa the Great, I'd have to trust him.

He pointed his wing inside to a hallway lit by torches.

"Welcome," croaked the white-eyed crow, "to the court of the Cat Sultan, Lord of the Cats, Ruler of the Two Lands and the Two Seas, Our Beloved Conqueror. All Hail the Cat Sultan."

Another crow appeared. Then another and another. They lined the walls, their dagger-sharp beaks blazing.

"Follow me." The crow pushed open a door to a bright chamber. I squinted, dazzled by a rush of sudden colour.

Everything in the room glowed with rich reds and deep greens. A glass chandelier lit the chamber. Sapphire blue tiles lined the walls and plush scarlet rugs patchworked the floor. Thick plumes of lavender-scented incense fogged the air. The chamber echoed with music and chattering laughter.

On one side of the room, three black-nosed sheep played drums and a flute. On the other side, six chubby chipmunks sucked on bubbling water pipes, their cheeks puffed up with smoke. The place was packed with all sorts of partying animals, all chattering and laughing among themselves, but there was no one who looked like a supernatural creature, at least not to me.

The crow pointed its wing across the room to a solid gold sofa covered with green silk pillows. On top of the sofa was an enormous orange cat. His fur was short and striped in places, tigerlike, and his round belly curved like he'd swallowed a gigantic egg. On his head, he wore a white turban decorated with a square emerald surrounded by a dozen shimmering pearls. Two brawny grey cats kneaded his shoulders.

The Cat Sultan held up a paw, and the music stopped instantly. A troupe of two dozen mice scurried out from under his chair and laced silk ropes around his waist, then hoisted him to a sitting position and propped him up with pillows. He settled into an imperious frown on top of a tubby mountain of orange fur.

"Karga, bring them here." The Cat Sultan eyed us darkly.

The big crow extended an oily-black wing and herded our group forwards.

I bowed my head and steadied my quivering voice. "If it pleases Your Highness – "

"I see you've brought me a gift." The Cat Sultan interrupted me. He extended his claws. Three chipmunks appeared and began filing them to a point.

I stared at him, confused. "A gift?"

"Looks tasty too," said the Cat Sultan.

"What is he talking about?" whispered Mina.

Azman shrugged like he was confused too.

"He's staring at me." Boz's whiskers quivered.

The Cat Sultan licked his lips and sank his eyes into Boz.

I leapt forwards. "No, Your Highness! This rat is our friend. We've come here to ask a favour. We need to find Mustafa the Great."

"You want a favour. I want a gift." The Cat Sultan tested the sharpness of his claws on a piece of fabric, slicing it to shreds.

Boz squeaked anxiously. "Let's get out of here!" He turned for the door.

"Nobody leaves the court without the Cat Sultan's permission," snarled Karga. A ring of crows tightened around us like a noose.

"But, but – " I scrambled for ideas, trying to stall. "We've brought you a different gift!"

"Yes! We have!" Mina leaned over and whispered to me. "What is it?"

I frantically rummaged through the corners of my brain. The Cat Sultan wouldn't want my good luck charm necklace. He had an emerald the size of a cream cracker pinned on his hat. Mina probably didn't have any money on her, and even if she did, it wouldn't be enough. We didn't have anything a Cat Sultan might want, except maybe –

"A show," I blurted out. "That's what Salyangoz had said, wasn't it? The Cat Sultan enjoyed entertainment – and he loved a good show."

Boz gaped at me. He knew exactly what I was thinking. "You can't be serious. I can't! I'll fail."

"You'll be great," I said.

The Cat Sultan slitted his eyes at us. "What kind of show?"

I swallowed. "A magic show, Your Highness, with Boz, the – the Super-Amazing Rat!"

The Cat Sultan sucked his teeth. "I do like magic shows, especially ones performed in my honour," he conceded. "I'll make you a deal. If I enjoy the show, I will let you all live."

There was no need to ask what he would do if he *didn't* enjoy the show. I swallowed hard. "If you enjoy it, will you promise to tell us where to find Mustafa the Great?"

The Cat Sultan tipped his whiskers at me, considering. "You make a lot of demands," he said. "Yes, I will make that promise, but it had better be a *very* good show."

"This is a terrible idea! We're all going to end up on the menu," Boz whispered to me.

Mina and Azman joined the huddle. "Do you have a better idea?" asked Mina.

Boz shook his head. "No, but . . ."

"Enough whispering." The Cat Sultan clapped his paws together. "Begin."

Boz's hands trembled as he reached into his hat and brought out his padlock. We watched nervously as Boz shuffled to the centre of the floor and bowed to the Cat Sultan. Boz held up a chain. It rattled with his quaking body. "I have here a steel chain." Boz glanced sideways at me. I mouthed the words, "You can do this", hoping to boost his confidence.

Boz squeaked something back to me, but I couldn't tell what he was saying.

He turned to the Cat Sultan. "This chain is strong enough to lift a three-sailed ship. It's stronger than the Byzantine chains that guarded the Golden Horn. I will now wrap myself in this chain and lock it tight, before I magically escape."

Boz looked over his shoulder and mouthed words to me again, this time more urgently: *extra key, hat.* I realized what he wanted me to do.

Boz held up a key. "And now, I will swallow the *one-and-only key* to this padlock." He dragged out the words 'one-and-only key' for dramatic effect, then opened his mouth and tossed in the key.

An awed chatter went up from the chamber's audience. While everyone was distracted, I slipped my paw into Boz's hat and fished around for the extra key. I caught it with a claw and pulled it out, then hid it between my toes.

"An escape artist! I love these shows," exclaimed the Cat Sultan.

Boz eyeballed me. "Now, I will require my assistant to help me put on the chains."

Boz beckoned to me. I swallowed hard, then stepped forwards and bowed like I was part of the performance. As soon as I got close, Boz whispered in my ear.

"Do you have the key?" he said.

I nodded.

He handed me one side of the chain as he began to turn, winding the chain around his middle until his arms were bound behind his back.

"As you can see, my assistant has tied the chains around my body. She will now lock them tight with this steel padlock."

I snapped the lock shut and gave it a yank, to show everyone that it was closed. As they looked at the lock, Boz opened his paw behind his back. I bowed again, the tiny key between my toes, as I edged closer to Boz and shoved my paw into his, releasing the key.

As I let go of it, Boz's trembling paw moved slightly and the key tumbled to the floor.

I gasped. *We're doomed. The Cat Sultan saw that, for sure.*

Before I could reach down to get it, Boz's foot shot out and stepped on the key. He plastered a smile on his face and checked the audience to see if anyone had noticed the extra key fall to the ground.

The Cat Sultan gazed at him expectantly. "Get on with it."

The Cat Sultan hadn't noticed. Nobody in the audience had. We might just get out of this alive.

Boz relaxed into a smile. "Yes! Let the magic begin."

He wiggled and squirmed, trying to get out of the chains. The audience watched enraptured as Boz groaned and twisted. After a few minutes, they pointed and tittered. The chipmunks, the mice, even the Cat Sultan sniggered. They were all laughing at him. I wanted to shout at them to be quiet. Boz dropped to the floor with a pained squeal. I leapt forwards to help him, but Mina grabbed me and held me tight.

"No! Wait. I know what he's doing," she said.

I turned to watch Boz. He was still writhing on the ground. But then – quick as lightning – he snatched the key I'd dropped on the ground and thrust it into the lock. It popped open with a clink and the chains slithered to the ground. The audience let out a delighted *Ahhhhh!* Their mouths still agape, Boz slyly slipped the key back into his jacket pocket.

Boz stood up and shouted: "TA-DA!"

He'd fallen on the ground intentionally. He'd made all that fuss so no one would notice when he picked up the key. It was *brilliant*. I let out a whoop of joy as I led the clamouring round of applause from the audience.

The Cat Sultan held up a paw and the clapping stopped. Silence filled the chamber as everyone waited to see what the Cat Sultan would say. He was quiet for a moment, then a wide grin spread across his face. He let out a hooting chuckle that shook his belly.

"Marvellous!" he bellowed.

They applauded again, and the Cat Sultan gestured for us to approach.

"You have held up your end of the bargain, so I will fulfil my promise. You seek Mustafa the Great, is that correct?"

asked the Cat Sultan.

My whiskers were still shaking from all the tension. "Yes, Your Highness."

"I assume you have heard that jinns like Mustafa are dangerous creatures," he said. "You visit at your own risk."

"Yes, Your Highness."

The Cat Sultan let his gaze linger over me like he was making a final decision. I tried to keep my heart from bursting through my chest.

"Mustafa appears at twilight on the summer solstice, which is tonight," he said. "You'll find him in the Sunken Palace at the Medusa's Head. But be aware: As soon as the sun sets and the moon rises, he will be gone."

A yelp of joy rushed from my throat. I knew where to find Mustafa the Great. I knew for sure where he was going to be!

"Karga will show you out," said the Cat Sultan. "You are all welcome at my court any time."

"Thank you, Your Highness." I offered a quick bow, then I raced for the door – with Mina, Boz and Azman close behind.

14
THE SCREECHING YOWL

The evening sun cast shadows across the avenue as Karga flew to a low-hanging branch of a fig tree. The crow pointed his wing west. "The Sunken Palace, where you will find Mustafa the Great, is located on the western side of the Hagia Sophia. Take this road until you come to a junction. Take a left at the narrow alley. You'll find a stone building with a wooden door. That is the entrance." He nodded his farewell, then took wing back to the Cat Sultan's court.

Mina tucked Boz in her pocket as we started down the cobblestone street. The air was sticky with wet humidity and my fur clung to my skin, but I didn't care. I shivered with a ripple of excitement. This could be it – I could be on my way *home*! If we could find Mustafa, I could ask him for help, and he might agree.

Azman turned left at a narrow alley, gesturing for us to follow him.

Boz poked his nose out of the top of the pocket. "Isn't anyone going to say it?"

I was distracted, thinking about Mustafa. "Isn't anyone going to say what?"

"That I was *spectacular*, of course. Did you see me? It was the best show I've ever done. I couldn't believe it!" said Boz.

"You did get a little help," said Mina.

"Yes, yes, I know. But Dalya dropped the key," Boz said. "They loved me! And – "

Mina bumped into Azman, who'd stopped. The fur on the back of his neck bristled as he lifted his nose to sniff.

"Why are we stopping?" asked Mina.

Her voice echoed in the empty alley. Clip-clopping horses and busy footsteps pounded in the street behind us, but we were alone here.

I held still and sniffed. Maybe the alley wasn't empty. There was a familiar scent in the air, but I couldn't place it. Where had I smelled that before?

Before I could work it out, something rustled behind me. I turned to look.

A burly squirrel stepped out of the shadows – the same one that had tracked us to the gold-crowned pigeon.

The squirrels. Again. Boz wasn't kidding when he said they were stubborn. These guys wouldn't give up! We didn't have time for this – I needed to find Mustafa *now* – or I was going to miss my chance to ask him for help.

The big squirrel had a potato sack over his shoulder. He tossed it to the ground and pulled back his lips in a snarl.

"Nice trick you pulled at the gate. It took us a while to work it out. Thought you'd outsmart us, did you?"

Three more squirrels appeared and formed a tight ring around us.

Azman shrank back with a whine, his quivering ears cowering against his head. He watched the big squirrel fearfully.

"You remember me, don't you?" The squirrel snapped his dagger-sharp teeth menacingly at Azman.

Azman flinched like he'd been trained to remember pain. The giant dog towered over the squirrels, and yet he looked terrified. It didn't make sense to me. What had they done to him when he was a puppy?

I glared at the squirrel. It didn't matter why Azman was scared – I wasn't going to let them frighten him anymore. There were four of us and four of them. Mina had her fists, Azman had his fangs, Boz was streetwise and I had retractable claws. We needed to fight them off.

I stepped in front of Azman. "Leave us alone."

Mina eyed me sideways, then followed my lead. "I already told you. This cat is not for sale, and you're not taking the dog either."

"Yeah! We won't let you take them." Boz nosed out from behind my leg and wagged a finger at them. "You shouldn't be selling cats and dogs for profit. That's animal cruelty!"

Only Azman was silent. His legs trembled.

"We're not here to bargain or debate. We're taking them both. This time, we brought reinforcements." The big squirrel opened his sack and grabbed a rope, then wound it up like he was holding a whip. His face dropped to an ugly sneer.

I clenched my teeth and arched my back, the hair on the scruff of my neck porcupining. He wasn't going to scare me so easily.

He snorted. "You really think you can escape again?"

"No. We're going to fight, and then you're going to leave us alone and never come back," I said.

"Is that right?" He laughed, then gave a loud whistle. Nothing happened for a moment. Then, the alleyway rumbled. The shadows bulged and loosened as two dozen squirrels materialized in the dark, tails rigid with anticipation.

Fifty black eyes pinned me to the spot. The squirrels' white teeth gleamed. We were outnumbered, out-clawed and out-toothed. Taunting the big squirrel had been a mistake. I should've been looking for a way to escape instead. I winced in instant regret.

"What's the matter? Don't have any more nuts to throw at us?" He reared up on his back legs and howled. *"Get them!"*

The squirrels launched into the air, claws open. One landed on my head and wrenched my whiskers. I tried to shake it off, but three more caught me by the tail and yanked as the big squirrel lassoed a rope around my neck.

I kicked as hard as I could with my hind legs, pummelling two squirrels on the neck and scratching a third across the cheek, but they kept coming at me, tightening the rope around my throat until I collapsed on my side.

Out of the corner of my eye I saw the squirrels thrust Boz

into a potato sack and tie it closed with a rope.

A dozen of them climbed up Mina's legs. They wrapped the rope around her arms and thighs, then jerked her to the ground.

Every inch of Azman's body twisted and writhed with a chaos of fur and claws, but he wasn't fighting them. He stood there, doing nothing, as they sank their teeth into his ears and tail. His gaze locked with mine, then he closed his eyes, like he was willing himself to move. He held still, breathing deep.

Then, an explosion of sound shattered the air like a clap of thunder. My skull rattled. There was a moment of stunned silence, and then a second eruption of noise. It was Azman – he was *barking*.

The squirrels whirled to face him. They stood on their hind legs, frozen, their mouths open in surprised terror.

Salyangoz had told us Azman hadn't made a sound since he'd been kidnapped by the squirrels as a puppy. But this wasn't just any sound. This was the loudest bark I'd ever heard. It shook the ground. It was the sound of a dog who could eat lions.

Azman's eyes blazed bright copper, and his shoulders stretched wide as a mountain. He opened his mouth and let out another earsplitting bark.

He got low and muscled towards the big squirrel. The other squirrels watched, stone still, paralysed.

"You're not going to hurt me," snarled the big squirrel. "You're still scared of me. I can tell."

"Go," growled Azman.

"Make me." The big squirrel bared his teeth.

He lunged at Azman – but Azman swerved left, then leapt forwards and clamped his jaws on the squirrel's back. The squirrel struggled furiously, scrabbling to escape.

"Let go of me, you useless mutt! I'll get you!" he screeched.

Azman shook the squirrel, then flung him against the alley wall. The squirrel struck the wall with a thud and slid down to the ground. He slumped over, eyes crossed, tail sagging. Azman had knocked him out.

Azman turned to the remaining squirrels. "Leave," he growled.

The squirrels blinked once in unison, still too frightened to move, before they chirped frantically – and then scattered away from us.

Azman used his teeth to untie my paws, then we both worked to untie Mina and Boz. We tossed the rope and sacks to the side. We were free.

Boz hopped to his feet and shook an angry fist at the fleeing squirrels. "Don't come back, you furry monsters! I'll tie your tails in knot!"

Mina wrapped her arms around Azman's neck. "You did it! You scared them away."

"Yes." Azman's voice was quiet and low – but he *had* a voice, and he was *using* it.

Boz smiled widely at him. "And you can talk."

Azman nodded shyly.

Boz joined the hug, then I did too. The four of us stood

together, shivering as we caught our breath.

Just as the alley was quiet again, we heard a voice.

"There she is." A potbellied man with thick stubble stood in a slant of light. I recognized him. He was the driver of the cart, the one who had picked up the wooden chest filled with Mina's gifts from her house.

Mina whipped around to face him. Next to him stood Aunt Sibel.

"Stay back." Mina whispered, gesturing to the shadows. "Hide."

"Ugh. Humans!" said Boz.

"*Bad* humans," I whispered back. If Aunt Sibel hated cats, she probably hated rats too. She didn't look like a dog person either.

"Is Mina going to be okay?" Boz asked.

I shook my head. I didn't know the answer. Worried fear squeezed my throat as I crouched down in the shadows, slinking closer to the people so I could hear what they were saying. Boz slouched towards the dark side of the alley and flattened against the wall, and Azman hid behind an oversized container, trying to make himself as small as possible.

Aunt Sibel stepped forwards and hovered over Mina, her eyes drawn to angry slits. She smiled like a shark, her teeth gleaming. "Thank you for finding my niece," she said, handing the man a fistful of coins.

"My pleasure." He pulled back his lips in a nasty smile as he bowed to leave. "I'll wait in the carriage."

Aunt Sibel turned to Mina. "Out wandering the streets, are we? Your father will hear about this."

Mina's chin quivered. Squirrel bites pockmarked her arms. She stood up and jutted her chin at the woman. "Yes, he will. I've already written him a letter and asked him to come home."

Aunt Sibel's face turned grey. For a split second, she looked worried, but then her face hardened again. "You did what?" she said.

Mina voice gained strength. "He's going to come home, and when he does, I'm going to tell him you're stealing everything he sends to me."

"You will do no such thing, you terrible, ungrateful child! I took care of you. I made food for you. I cleaned up after you. Your father *owed* me that money," Aunt Sibel snarled. "When he comes home, you're not going to tell him anything."

Aunt Sibel snatched Mina up by the collar and she dangled like a ragdoll. "I know how you got out of the house yesterday: You climbed down the vines. That was very dangerous. Naughty little girls shouldn't do things like that. You could have an unfortunate 'accident'.

"You wouldn't hurt me," said Mina.

"Wouldn't I? Are you certain?" Aunt Sibel hissed, flecks of spittle hitting Mina. "I'll tell your father I tried to stop you, that I begged you not to do dangerous things, but you wouldn't listen. I'll say it was a tragedy but there was nothing anyone could do . . . when you *fell from the window*."

Mina whimpered.

Accident? Tragedy? I quickly replayed every word I'd heard, trying to make sure I understood, but I didn't want to believe it. Aunt Sibel meant to *hurt* Mina.

Rage exploded in my chest. I rocketed forwards in a blur of white.

Before I could get there, Aunt Sibel grabbed Mina by the neck and jerked her into the horse carriage. The door slammed behind them as the driver cracked the whip – and galloped away with Mina.

In a burst of desperate fury, I let loose a screeching yowl. "Azman! Boz! She's taking Mina away!"

I turned to look, but they weren't moving.

"Come on," I yowled. "We don't have time to waste. We have to save Mina."

Boz and Azman exchanged glances.

"What are you waiting for?" I demanded.

"Azman and I will find a way to help Mina," said Boz.

"What are you talking about? We don't have time for this! We have to go after Mina right now," I said.

"*You* need to leave now to find Mustafa, or you'll never get back home. The sun will set soon. If you don't get to the Sunken Palace before the moon rises, you'll be trapped here," said Boz.

Azman nodded his agreement.

I knew what Boz was saying was true, but I didn't care. "This is my fault. If I hadn't told her she had to leave the house, if I hadn't said anything about the cupboard – " I couldn't stop shaking.

Zehra Hala said I was supposed to set things right – that I was the "family secret" – but all I'd done since I arrived was make things worse. Now Mina was in danger. And for what? Because I'd got angry with Baba and made a stupid wish? I never should've followed that cat upstairs. It was silly and wrong, and I should've known better.

Mina had risked everything for me. When I'd told her that she needed to be a friend and help me, she'd done it. I couldn't leave her like this.

My stomach hollowed out like I was plummeting over a cliff. I tried to stop my mind from churning. There *had* to be a way to fix this.

I set my jaw and turned to Boz. "We still have time. We'll go to the house, break her out and then come back here. If we hurry, we can do it before the moon rises."

Boz and Azman exchanged another worried glance.

"That's a big risk, Dalya," said Boz.

"She's going to *hurt Mina*," I said.

The longer we stood there arguing, the less chance we had of saving her in time.

"I have to do this," I pleaded. "When you asked to come along, Boz, you promised you'd help me."

Boz scratched his chin thoughtfully. "I did make a promise. I also told you rats were clever, and this is not a clever plan. It's brave, but not clever."

"Please, Boz." My whiskers quivered.

He let out a sigh.

"You make it very hard to say no, you know that?"

I brightened a little. "So, you'll help me?"

He nodded reluctantly. "It'll be faster if we go down to the main road. We'll sneak onto a cart going across the bridge."

Azman darted in front of us and lay down with a whine. "Climb on."

"But why sneak onto a cart when you have a dog as big as a lion?" Boz smiled, then shook his head. "There's no way this is going to work."

"Yes, it will. It has to." I climbed up onto Azman's back and the massive dog lurched forwards.

15
THE DANGEROUS PLAN

The sun dipped towards the horizon like a gleaming penny as we rounded the corner into the mansion courtyard. The silhouetted shape of Mina perched in the first-floor window, her form shuddering like she was crying. We crouched behind a bush, watching her.

The first-floor window that Mina and I had used the day before was boarded up. Since Aunt Sibel had worked out how we'd got out of the house, she'd clearly decided to make sure we never did it again. If we couldn't use that window, though, it meant we'd have to get the keys from Aunt Sibel.

The trouble was, Aunt Sibel wore the keys around her neck.

I scanned the house, looking for a way inside. My gaze stopped when I got to the attic window. It was high above the ground, near the roof, and it was open.

A plan began to form in my mind. It was dangerous, but it might work. I tapped Boz on the shoulder and pointed to a tree.

"Boz, do you see that tree branch above the back door? I need you to climb it and wait there," I said.

"For what?"

"We have to steal the keys from around Aunt Sibel's neck. Can you do it?"

"Of course I can, but I still don't understand. What are you going to do?"

"Just be ready when she comes outside." I turned to Azman. "As soon as Boz has the keys, I need you to scare Aunt Sibel away from the house, into the courtyard."

He nodded and then pulled back his lips, making a show of baring his teeth.

"Yes. Exactly like that. You're terrifying," I said.

Azman grinned, pleased with himself.

"Are we ready?" I asked.

Boz and Azman nodded.

I sank my claws into the vines along the side of the house and began climbing up slowly.

Boz followed my intended path to the open attic window. "Wait a second. You're not going all the way up there, are you? That's too high! It won't matter if you land on four feet from that height. You'll break your legs."

I wasn't sure if he was right, but we didn't have time to come up with a better plan. I paused and took a deep breath. "Just be ready," I called over my shoulder.

I flexed my claws, digging them into the tangled ivy as I pushed with my hind legs and continued scaling the side of the house, paw over paw.

My muscles quivered. Cats were good climbers, but I'd

never seen one go straight up the side of a house. I shook the doubts from my mind. *I can do this.* If I wanted to save Mina, I was going to have to. I reached out my paw and continued climbing.

The vines were thick on the ground and first floors, but they thinned near the second floor. There was barely enough ivy for me to hang on to. I looked at the horizon. The air had begun to cool as the sky dimmed to a dusky orange. It was getting late. I'd have to move faster if I was going to rescue Mina and get back to Mustafa in time. I hurried up towards the attic.

I was getting close, which was a good thing because I didn't know how much longer I could hold on. *The window is just a few metres away*, I told myself. *You can do this.*

As I reached out a paw for the windowsill, I heard a ripping sound. *Oh no.*

A clump of ivy tore away from the side of the house.

I screeched as I swung in the air, barely holding on with one paw, clawing frantically with the other, my hind legs scratching at the wood siding – until I hooked my claws on the windowsill and dug in.

I dangled in the air, holding on with one paw. A chilly breeze ruffled the fur on my stomach. My lungs felt like they were melting inside me – I could hardly breathe.

Boz was too far away for me to hear exactly what he was saying, but he was squeaking wildly.

I quietened my thoughts, forcing myself to focus. "I can do this," I whispered to myself.

With one last push, I pulled myself onto the ledge, then sat there, my whole body shaking. I tipped my face over the ledge to wave to Boz and show him I was okay, but I pulled back quickly when I saw how far up I was. The attic was dizzyingly high. If I'd fallen . . . I didn't want to admit Boz was right. I couldn't let myself think about what could have happened.

I wriggled through the open window and landed quietly on the attic floor, then padded towards a staircase that went down to the first floor. At the bottom of the stairs, I stopped and listened. The faint sound of Mina's sniffles filtered down the hallway from her bedroom. Fainter still, I could hear the quick, angry footsteps of Aunt Sibel on the ground floor. She was in the kitchen, right where I wanted her.

Getting inside the house through the attic window turned out to be the easy part of the plan. Now came the tricky part. I straightened my whiskers and steadied my breathing before stepping forwards.

Moving quietly through the hallway, past Mina's room, I made my way down the staircase to the kitchen. There she was. Aunt Sibel had her back turned to me.

There was only one way my plan could work. I needed to be scary. I squeezed my eyes shut and took a deep breath, puffing up my chest as much as I could, before I moved into the light, arched my back, and made a noise that sounded something like a hiss and something like an angry goat. Not exactly scary, but at least it was loud.

Aunt Sibel dropped her teacup and whipped around to face

me. A rash of red rage crawled up her neck. "You again," she snarled. "This time, you won't get away!"

I opened my mouth to shout back at her, but all that came out was a screeching yowl.

She snatched the broom from the cupboard and held it above her head like a battleaxe as she swiped at me, but I swerved left and leapt onto the worktop. She shot forwards to grab me as I sprinted past the sink. My left hind leg slipped on the slick worktop, sending dirty dishes clattering into the metal sink. I led her across the room, towards the back door, where I screeched to a halt and twirled around to face her.

She stood next to the back door. I needed to get her outside the house so we could rescue Mina, and I had a plan: Make her sneeze.

I arched my back and hissed again, creeping closer to her. She grimaced menacingly, but I didn't care. I tensed my muscles and launched myself directly at her chest, digging my claws into the fancy fabric of her purple dress.

She tried to pry me off, but I held on. "Get off me!" she shouted.

Just as she opened her mouth to shout, I rubbed my furry cheeks on her nose.

Aunt Sibel's eyes bulged. She coughed and spluttered, using the back of her sleeve to rub the fur off her nose. She reeled back to sneeze. Just before she let loose, I leapt onto her head and dug my claws into her hair. She stumbled towards the door.

"You disgusting animal!" she yelped. "Get out of here!"

She sneezed again as she opened the back door and we tumbled outside. Scrambling to her feet, she caught me by the neck and pulled me off her head, then flung me into the shrubbery. I soared through the air – the wind whistling through my whiskers – and landed neatly on four feet.

Perfect. I turned and smirked at Aunt Sibel. She was hunched over, hacking and snorting. Now for the next part of our plan.

Aunt Sibel turned to go back inside, but before she got to the door, Boz dropped from the tree branch above her and squeezed under the collar of her dress. She screamed, writhing and twisting as he squirmed past her waist and down her leg, then out of the bottom of her dress. He raced to the bushes as she stomped after him, furiously trying to squash him.

"I've got the keys!" shouted Boz.

Then he let out a deafening squeak.

Aunt Sibel had him by the tail and was holding him upside down. She drew a jewelled hatpin from her hair and held it like a dagger. She pulled back, ready to stab Boz.

"Azman! Dalya! Help!" Boz squealed.

Azman lunged for at Aunt Sibel, a rumbling growl vibrating in his throat.

Aunt Sibel's face went white as she began backing away. "Nice doggy."

He bared his teeth. She let out a pathetic whimper as she dropped Boz to the ground. He scampered to my side.

Azman crept closer to Aunt Sibel, herding her away from the back door, just like we'd planned. As soon as she was far enough away, I called out to him.

"Let's go!" I said.

Azman stopped growling at Aunt Sibel and turned. We darted inside the house, and Azman shouldered the door shut. Boz scampered up Azman's back and locked the door . . . with Aunt Sibel trapped outside.

She banged against the door, shouting, but we had the keys.

We slumped together for a moment, huffing and trembling in silence. We'd done it, and it had gone almost perfectly. At least, so far.

I grinned at Boz. "See? That wasn't too hard."

"Easy for you to say. You're not the one who almost got stuck in Aunt Sibel's underwear. I'm going to need to get my whiskers sanitized." He sniffed himself and made a sour face.

"That was pretty amazing how you got the keys from her. Only a real magician could've pulled that off," I said.

"You're just trying to make me feel better," he said.

"Is it working?"

He brightened. "A little bit. Maybe."

I laughed and patted him on the back. "Good. Now, let's go and get Mina."

We quickly made our way upstairs to Mina's bedroom. Boz rifled through the keys, trying one after another, until one of them fitted and the door clicked open. Mina jumped up from her bed as I sprang into her arms.

"You came back for me." Mina gave me an appreciative hug, then her face turned serious. "That wasn't very smart, Dalya."

I rubbed my cheek against Mina's, purring. "I couldn't let Aunt Sibel do anything to you."

"Thank you," she whispered, holding me tight.

Boz climbed up onto a basket and looked outside to see the last pink of twilight light the sky. "We need to get going."

Mina nodded. She stood up, blew out the oil lamp, and pulled back the curtain to peek out. "I can't see Aunt Sibel. She probably went to the neighbour's house."

"I hope you're right. Everyone ready?" Boz unlocked the door. The door swung open as we cautiously looked around the courtyard. The shadows were dark and quiet. Mina threw her leg over Azman's back like a horse and wrapped her arms around his neck. I hopped into her lap as she tucked Boz into her pocket.

"Ready," she said.

Azman slunk out the door into the courtyard.

Mina whispered in his ear. "I think we're safe."

Azman started at a trot, then went faster into a gallop. As he rounded the corner out of the courtyard, he skidded to halt.

Aunt Sibel jumped in front of him, clutching her broom.

"You wicked child!" Aunt Sibel raised the broom to hit Mina, but Mina's hand shot out and grabbed it from her.

Mina held it for a moment, her cheeks flaming, her eyes digging into Aunt Sibel's.

They stared at each other as the rest of us held our breath.

When I'd first met Mina, she'd been terrified of Aunt Sibel. She'd seemed so small compared to the woman, and I remembered her chin wobbling as Aunt Sibel thundered at her.

Mina seemed bigger now, somehow – straighter and taller. Her chin no longer wobbled.

"Don't ever hit me again." Mina's voice was firm. "And don't you *dare* hurt my friends." Mina tossed the broom on the ground.

"I say we lock her up properly," squeaked Boz.

"I agree." Mina slid off Azman and turned to Aunt Sibel. "Go inside. Now."

Aunt Sibel snorted. "You can't tell me what to do."

Azman growled.

"Yes, I can," said Mina.

Azman bared his teeth at Aunt Sibel. I did too, and so did Boz.

"You made me believe my father didn't care about me, and all the while you were *stealing*," said Mina.

Aunt Sibel's gaze flicked from face to face as she backed away from us. "Please, Mina. You can't tell your father about this. He'll kick me out of the house. I don't have anywhere to go."

"You should've thought about that before you lied to me," said Mina.

"But I did everything for you, Mina. I took care of you," Aunt Sibel whined.

Mina didn't say anything.

She drew her mouth into a firm line and pointed.

"Go inside. Now," said Mina. "My father will deal with you later."

Azman shoved Aunt Sibel with his snout. Aunt Sibel tripped forwards, then turned to scowl at us, but she was outnumbered. There was no way for her to escape.

"I'm warning you, Aunt Sibel. Do as I say," said Mina.

Aunt Sibel nodded weakly. She was defeated. Slowly she turned towards the house. We herded her up to her room, which was littered with dirty dishes again.

"Do you still have the key, Boz?" asked Mina.

"Yes, I do." He held it up.

Mina waited until Aunt Sibel was inside the room and then thrust the key into the door. She locked it with a satisfying clunk, then looped the keychain around her neck for safekeeping.

"Please don't leave me locked in here!" Aunt Sibel let out a muffled cry from behind the locked door. The last thing we heard were Aunt Sibel's shouts as the four of us sprinted away from the house and down the street with no one to stop us.

Azman's thick legs pounded the ground. We held on tight, our bodies colliding with air, buildings pouring past us as we flew like an arrow. The light faded to a cold grey. Azman pushed harder, going faster, mouth foaming, racing, but the stars were already showing their faces. The full moon hovered on the horizon like a silver eye. There wasn't much time left.

As we rounded the corner and slid to a halt, joy flooded my veins. *We'd made it.*

"Over there!" I pointed to the building across from the south corner of Hagia Sophia, where Karga had told us to find the entrance to the Sunken Palace. This had to be it.

The old stone building was small, with an even smaller wooden door. Moss dripped from its walls, and tree branches spread their fingers over its clay roof. It didn't look like a palace at all. I couldn't guess why a powerful jinn would pick a place like this. A flickering doubt sparked in my mind. Maybe he wasn't so powerful after all. If he'd turned me into a cat, though, he had to have some magic. Didn't he?

Shaking off my misgivings, I hopped off Azman's back and darted across the street, then stood up on my hind legs and pushed against the door with my paws.

It wouldn't open. I tried again, then again. The door remained shut.

"Mina, I need you!" I called. "Open this door. Hurry!"

Mina rattled the door handle. It was locked.

"Hello?" I called out. "Bang on the door, Mina. Maybe he's still inside. Maybe he can hear us."

Mina banged, and Boz joined in, scratching his paws on the wood as I called *hello* over and over again. There was no answer.

"Open the door!" I pounded against it, wishing for fists instead of paws. "Why are you stopping? We have to make him hear us!"

"Dalya," said Mina.

I whirled around. "What?"

She pointed to the sky. A lighted crescent peeked above

the tree line. My ears cast triangle moon shadows on the cobblestone street. If I could see the moon, it meant Mustafa the Great was gone, which meant . . .

My stomach folded into knots. *No, this couldn't be happening.* I threw my shoulder against the door again, willing it to open, still hoping against hope.

But I already knew the truth. We were too late. I'd failed.

Everything in my body went cold and my legs crumpled underneath me. I'd known it was risky to try to save Mina, but I'd still thought we'd make it somehow. We were *so close.*

When I'd rubbed the magic bottle, I'd wanted to disappear so I could teach Baba a lesson. I was angry and wanted to hurt him, but I wished I'd been patient, like he'd asked. My heart felt like it was being squeezed between two boulders, so tightly I could hardly breathe. My whiskers quivered as I crouched down, tail tucked, making myself as small as possible.

Nothing mattered now. The only thing I'd wanted was to go home, and I was too late. Mina, Boz and Azman sat quietly beside me as a hot tear slid down my nose.

16

THE SUNKEN PALACE

A fizzing sound crackled in my ear. I glanced down at my tail. It was glowing again, sparkling as if it was covered with twinkling stars. Golden dust scattered on the polished granite before it liquified into molten metal. The glistening drops swirled around each other like a galaxy, spinning closer and closer until they formed a solid, round circle. A cat's paw print appeared in the middle of the golden circle, gleaming blue and then yellow, then blue again. The same colours as my eyes.

"What is that?" asked Mina.

"I have no idea," I said.

I stared at it for a moment, trying to guess what it could be. It was raised around the edges, like some sort of *button*. What was it for?

"Maybe you're supposed to touch the paw print," said Mina.

Boz scratched his chin. "It could be a trap."

There was only one way to find out. I ventured a paw and placed it in the centre. The metallic button sank into the stone and disappeared with a white flash. I pulled back, shading my eyes.

Everything was quiet. Then, with a long creak, the Sunken Palace door swung open.

My pulse skipped. The button wasn't a trap. It controlled the door. *We were in!* I held out hope that Mustafa hadn't left yet – that we could find him, somehow.

I nosed through the door and looked around. It was completely dark, but as soon as I took a step inside, a torch lit itself on the opposite wall. Mina, Boz and Azman trailed after me, and the door creaked shut behind us. There was no going back now.

We stood at the top of a staircase. The rock steps were steep and cut straight down, but it was too dark to see where they went. The air smelled wet and earthy, like a freshwater lake. As I stepped on the first stair, another torch lit itself. Then another and another lit up, all the way down, following us as we descended into the hollow deep.

Just before we got to the bottom of the stairs, we stopped to look around. We were inside a wide underground cavern. Ancient marble columns crisscrossed the cavern like a chessboard. Between each one stretched a high, rounded arch decorated with a mosaic of multicoloured bricks. A steady *drip-drip* echoed in the silence.

I glanced down at the floor. It was shiny and wet. I reached down and touched it with my paw. It wasn't a floor at all – it was glassy, smooth water, black as midnight, flickering with the reflected light of the torches.

The Sunken Palace. I'd wondered why they'd given it that name, but now it made sense. The place looked as though it had once housed a magnificent underground kingdom that had long ago been flooded and abandoned.

Unless we wanted to swim, though, we were stuck on the stairs. We had no idea how deep the water was, or how big the cavern might be. We didn't even know where we wanted to go. The stairs had led us to a dead end.

"Hello?" I called out. My voice disappeared in the dark. There was no answer. I turned to Mina, Boz and Azman. "How are we going to find Mustafa?"

"I don't know," said Mina.

"I've heard stories about this place," said Boz. "No one knows exactly how or when it was built, but there are rumours it was once home to a magical queen."

"A nice queen?" Mina's voice shook a little.

"If she lived in a cave, I doubt it," said Boz.

"*Shh,*" I hushed. "I hear something."

From far away in the blackness came a bubbly popping noise. It was the same sound my own tail made when it sparkled – the same sound I'd heard when I saw the cat in the window that first night in Zehra Hala's house. But the sound wasn't coming from *my* tail, which could only mean one thing.

The mysterious cat, the one who had got me into this mess, had to be here somewhere.

I rotated my ears this way and that as my brain cranked, listening to the dank, chill air, trying to pinpoint the location.

The cat had led me to the magic bottle. Maybe now it would lead me to Mustafa. I just had to work out a way to follow the sound.

Then, below us, under the water, a light began to glow. With a rush of churning bubbles, a golden rowing boat floated from the bottom to the surface. The seats were perfectly dry, as if the boat had never been submerged.

The four of us exchanged astonished glances.

"Do you think it's safe?" asked Mina.

"Unlikely," said Boz.

"We don't have a choice." I put one paw in the boat. It held steady. Boz was right: It probably wasn't safe, but there was no turning back now. I jumped into the boat. "Come on."

Mina followed me, then Azman and Boz. As soon as we were seated, the boat began to glide across the water, as if it were being pulled by an invisible rope. We turned left and right, then right again, going deeper and deeper into the cavern. The fizzing sounds got louder and louder until the boat came to a stop and a dozen torches lit up all at once.

I put my paws on the edge of the boat to look around. We were floating in front of a wide stone column. At the base was an upside-down statue of a woman's head. She had a sad smile and blank eyes. Green moss slicked her face, and her stone hair coiled with frozen snakes. *The Upside-Down Medusa.* This was where the Cat Sultan told us we were supposed to meet Mustafa the Great. I glanced around anxiously. He should be here.

With a hissing sound, two eyes flamed to life in the dark, one blue and one yellow. My blood felt like it had stopped pumping, as if it had turned to ice inside my veins.

The eyes leapt on top of the statue's chin and stepped into the light. Whiskers appeared, and then a tail. It *was* the cat I'd followed upstairs. It hooked its gaze into mine as it swished its tail, sending a wisp of glittery dust into the air that swirled and whirled, growing in size until it became a tiny glimmering tornado. I was dazzled by the sudden light, but I forced myself to look so I could see what was happening.

Inside the shimmering whirlwind, the cat's white whiskers sprouted into a man's grey beard. His paws lengthened to arms, and his claws stretched into bony fingers. The dust materialized into a red velvet robe embroidered with golden thread. His triangle cat ears melded together to form a pointy hat trimmed in black-and-white fur. The only thing about him that stayed the same were his blazing blue and yellow eyes.

He stepped onto a golden disc that floated on top of the water in front of the Medusa statue. He towered over us, his gaze moving from one face to the next as if he were examining and judging each one of us.

"Welcome, friends." His voice tinkled like a wind chime. "I'm delighted to see you all here. I assume you are here to ask for wishes."

He was asking about wishes, and jinns were supposed to grant wishes, so this *had* to be Mustafa the Great.

I clamped my teeth shut, trying to keep my heart from flying out. When we'd found the door to the Sunken Palace locked, I was sure we were too late – but I'd found him! My pulse sped up with anticipation.

"Yes," I spluttered. "I do have a wish. I'd like to go home."

Mustafa looked me over. "No," he said flatly.

I blinked at him. This was exactly what I'd been worried about – he wasn't going to help me.

"Even if I wanted to help you," he continued. "I couldn't. Like all magical creatures, jinns are bound by rules. I can't grant wishes that have already come true."

Already come true? That made no sense. "I don't understand," I said.

"Let's start with you, Mina. What was it that you wanted?" asked Mustafa.

Mina issued me a sideways glance as she stuttered. "I-I wished for a friend."

"Have you found any that are suitable?" He gestured broadly to all of us.

Mina glanced at Azman, Boz and me. "Well, yes. I've found some lovely friends."

"It's true that I helped you meet Dalya, but you were the one who turned her into a friend. You did that on your own. You didn't need magic. You have proved a loyal companion, and you've been rewarded with friendship in return. You made your own wish come true," said Mustafa.

Mustafa turned to Azman. "I understand you've given up your shyness and found your bark again. That was some marvellous noise you made in the alleyway. You managed to save your friends from the squirrels. That courage was all your own," said Mustafa.

Azman whined and nodded. "Yes."

"How about you, Boz? You wanted to be a successful magician. I thought your trick went rather well at the Cat Sultan's court. All you needed was an assistant," said Mustafa. "Am I wrong?"

Boz blinked at him. "Well, no, but – "

Mustafa shrugged. "See? All done."

Boz's mouth gaped open. "Wait a second. How did you know all of this?"

"Magic is best left a mystery, Mister Rat. Now, if you'll kindly hand over my bottle, I'll be leaving. You were late, my dear. The moon is high. I should already be gone." He held out his hand expectantly. "My bottle, please."

I couldn't move. I held still, trying to process everything he'd just said. "But . . . I want to go home."

"Yes, so you said when you made your wish. But you were not specific about what 'home' meant to you."

That was ridiculous. He had to have known what I meant. I cleared my throat and spoke clearly to make sure he understood me this time. "I don't want to be a cat anymore. I want to see my dad again."

"In Istanbul," he said.

"Yes," I answered.

"So that's 'home'?" he asked.

No, it wasn't. It was where my dad was. Not always, but just for now. That's where I wanted to go. I wanted to be with Baba.

I glared at him. He was trying to trick me into saying the wrong thing again. This was going to be harder than I thought. If I wanted to get back to Baba, I was going to have to outsmart this jinn, and I had no idea how I was going to do it.

"You can see, now, why this is complicated," he said.

Actually, *he* was the one complicating things. "You're not being fair. I read the riddle. There was nothing in there about turning into a cat."

"Ah yes. The cat part was my own touch. Being a feline is such a wonderful adventure. So many interesting smells and sounds, and you get to be such a beautiful creature. Don't you agree?"

"I don't," I said firmly. "You did this to me. You have to fix it."

"That's another rule: I can't undo rubs of the magic bottle. A rub is a rub, I'm afraid," he said. "I grow annoyed with you all. Hand it over."

"You're really not going to help me?" I asked.

"No."

I crouched down, suddenly dizzy. I'd known there was a possibility he wouldn't grant my request, but somehow, I'd still hoped he would. Until now.

"Shame on you," Mina said to Mustafa. "We've spent days trying to find you!"

"*The bottle.*" Mustafa scowled. "I need it."

I snorted angrily. That was perfect, just perfect. I'd come all this way for nothing. He wouldn't lift a finger to help me, yet he wanted me to hand over his bottle?

Wait a second. How badly did he need it?

I had an idea, a daring one, but it might work. "You're eager to get your bottle back." I measured my words carefully.

"And?" he said.

"I saw you at Zehra Hala's house. I followed you upstairs to the first floor. Why didn't you take the bottle then?" I asked.

"I can't take it back myself," he said. "That's another rule. A bottle has to be freely given."

"Is that why you sent me on this adventure? So I'd bring your bottle back?" I asked.

Silence filled the Sunken Palace, and I knew I was on the right track. I tapped my tail against the bottom of the boat impatiently.

"Technically, you did this to yourself by meddling with magic." He sniffed. "I suppose I encouraged you a little. Yes, that's why I did it. I needed my bottle back."

A smile crept across my lips. There *was* a way to outsmart him, and this was it! I tilted my whiskers at him and strengthened my voice. "I won't give it back unless you help me get home."

Mustafa expelled a laugh. "I admire your determination, Dalya. I truly do."

"It's a fair trade. My home for yours," I said.

He quietened his laughter, then looked me over like he was making a decision. "All right. I'll make you a deal: I will help you get home, but you must first pass a test."

It was risky striking a bargain with a jinn. If I'd learned one thing in the last few days, that was it. I cautiously nodded my agreement.

"Then let's begin the test. Come," he beckoned.

Mustafa moved his hands like he was pulling an invisible rope. As he did, sparkling dust lifted out of the water and gathered together into a solid golden bridge.

I cautiously placed one paw on it, then padded across it to the floating, golden disc where Mustafa stood. Mustafa fished a piece of yellowed paper from one of his sleeves and a quill pen from the other, then he dipped the quill into the water.

"You came here by way of a magic ink, and that is how you must exit." The paper unrolled itself and floated in the air as the quill hovered over it like it was waiting for instruction.

"What am I supposed to do?" I asked.

"I'm going to ask you some questions, and the quill will record your answers. I want to see if you have learned what 'home' truly means."

"I don't understand." This test didn't make any sense.

"By the end, you will understand. I promise."

I frowned. If I couldn't understand the purpose of the test, there was no way I was going to pass it.

He tipped his head at me. "Do you want to try?"

I didn't have much of a choice, did I? I nodded.

"Good. Now, look into the water. What do you see?"

I looked down at the glassy black water and was astonished to see myself – not my cat self, but my *real* self. I gasped with joy, touching my face, then looked back down at my hands – they were still paws. My smile crumbled. He was playing another trick on me. I bristled my whiskers at the jinn and grimaced.

"Be patient," he said. "Answer the question. Tell the quill what you see."

What was the point of this? I still didn't understand. I faced the water again and looked. "I see dark hair, hazel eyes. Dark eyelashes. I'm wearing my favourite T-shirt."

The quill pen scratched at the paper, constructing an eerily accurate image of my human self.

"Is that all?" Mustafa's smile soured as he reached out to collect his quill and parchment.

"Wait!" I said.

He halted.

I looked closer. The blue eye necklace Zehra Hala had given me glinted in the firelight. It hung around my neck. I touched it with my paw.

My vision blurred, and Baba's face appeared. As it did, our eyes overlapped in the watery reflection, and my breath caught. When Zehra Hala had given me the necklace, she'd told me I looked like Baba and I hadn't believed her. I'd thought I wasn't anything like him, but it wasn't true. I could see it now. We both had hazel eyes with thick black lashes, and the corners of our eyes turned up at the sides.

Two more faces appeared behind my Baba: Zehra Hala and Mina. All four of us were there together in the mirror, talking and laughing. All of us had the same eyes, and we looked like we belonged together. Not just because we were physically similar – there was something more. We fitted together like a family.

My family.

As my vision cleared and the faces began to disappear, a sense of certainty settled in my chest. When I got back, things would change. I'd tell Baba how much I missed him. That I understood he had to work, and I could be patient. That I was willing to try to reconnect with him.

"What else do you see?" asked Mustafa.

"I'm wearing a blue eye necklace," I said. "It's been in my family for a long time."

"*Your* family?" he asked.

My eyes turned to find Mina. A swell of pride rose in my chest. She'd proved a brave and loyal friend, and she'd found the courage to tell her father about Aunt Sibel. As Mina smiled, the torchlight caught her face, and I smiled back.

Salyangoz had said I'd learn something true and real about myself while I was here, and he was right. I belonged to this family, and they belonged to me.

I nodded to Mustafa slowly and deliberately. "Yes, *my* family."

"Now, tell me. What does 'home' mean to you, Dalya?"

Zehra Hala's words surfaced in my mind. "*Any place can be home if you keep an open heart.*" She'd said that to me on the first morning I arrived in Istanbul.

"Home isn't a place. It's wherever you find friendship and

love," I said. Love, friendship – and family. That was my *real* home. That's what it meant to me. "I want to go home to my Baba."

The quill stopped moving, and the parchment rolled itself up. Mustafa bowed to me, then tied a red ribbon around the parchment and handed it to me.

"I passed the test? I can go now?" I asked.

"Yes." He smiled. "Whenever you are ready, you may go."

I hesitated. There was one more thing I wanted to ask. "The riddle said I was the family secret. Zehra Hala said so too. What does it mean?"

"Every child is the family secret, Dalya. You are the real magic in this world because you contain both the past and the future. A thousand generations of your family's kisses and hopes made you, all the way back to the beginning of time. Their love runs through your veins and binds you to each and every one of them, even if you don't know it, no matter how far away you are in space or time, forever. You are the answer to every wish they ever made – that is who you are." He touched my cheek.

I turned his words over in my mind, holding them there for a moment, feeling their weight like stones.

"And now, Dalya, you should take some time to say farewell to your friends before you leave," said Mustafa.

"Wait. You can't forget to take your bottle," I said.

"Ah, yes!" he said.

I used my teeth to undo the knot from my collar, then I

opened the bundle and pawed the ink bottle over to him.

"Oh, how I've missed my lovely bottle!" Mustafa exclaimed. "I have hundreds of them, but this one has always been my favourite. It's roomy inside, and I designed all the furniture myself." Mustafa pocketed the magic bottle with a satisfied grin.

"There is one more person that Mina must meet. Perhaps you would like to go with her," said Mustafa.

"Yes, thank you. I'd like that very much," I said.

He nodded to me. "After all your farewells are said, open the scroll, and you will find your way home."

I paced down the bridge to rejoin my friends on the boat. We waved goodbye to Mustafa as we drifted down a dark tunnel that opened onto the starry night.

The boat stopped at the end of a wooden pier. A tall figure with a mustache and a turban waited for us next to three white cranes.

"*Baba!*" Mina leapt out of the boat and bounded into his arms.

He offered a merry laugh and picked her up to twirl her around. Mina giggled with glee. When he set her down, he stopped for a moment and peered at her face. A bruise had just begun to purple her cheek where Aunt Sibel had slapped her. He gently traced his finger over it.

"Who do this to you?" he asked.

"Aunt Sibel."

He hugged Mina tight. "I'm so sorry, Mina. I didn't know until I got your letter. I should've come home sooner."

"I should've asked you to come home sooner," said Mina. "She's been lying to you. She lied to both of us."

There was something about Mina's father that reminded me of Baba. He had the same crooked smile, the same hazel eyes.

Mina took his hand and led him towards me. "These are my friends. This is Dalya, this is Boz and this is Azman."

He offered us a deep bow. We bowed back as he kneeled down next to Mina. "You are wise beyond your years, my little one. They say there is a reward in heaven for every act of kindness done to a living animal."

"These animals have done me a kindness." Mina leaned her forehead on his. "They helped *me*. They all did."

"Then they will be welcome in our house whenever they please," he said.

"Can they come and live with us?" asked Mina.

He laughed. "We'll see about that."

"They'll be good, Baba, I promise!" said Mina. Azman whined happily. Boz squeaked and leapt onto Mina's shoulder as she laughed.

As I watched Mina smile, I could feel the warmth spreading through my body. She had been so lonely when I'd met her. Now she was happy, and I was happy for her.

Mina's father gave her another hug. "Stay here. I'll go and get the carriage," he said.

Mina smiled at me. "I suspect you'd like to see your own father now."

It was true. I couldn't wait to see my Baba. I wanted to feel his warmth and smell his aftershave and hug him as much as I could.

Mina, Boz and Azman gathered around me.

"I guess this is goodbye." I couldn't believe I was really going home. It had been such a crazy journey, with so many ups and downs. I was lucky to have met such special friends and I was going miss each one of them.

Azman leaned down and nuzzled my neck. I rubbed my cheek against his nose. "Thank you for saving me from the squirrels." He nodded solemnly to me, then stepped back.

Boz pulled a handkerchief out of his pocket and blew his nose. "Don't be sad, Boz," I said. "You're a talented magician, and I know you'll get a new assistant soon."

"Not one as good as you." He wrapped his paws around my neck, and I patted his back.

I turned to Mina last. She wrapped her arms around me as I pitched forwards and purred. We held each other for a long moment. I wanted to tell her who I was, but I still didn't know how.

I leaned my cheek against hers and whispered in her ear. "I'll miss you."

"Me too," she whispered back.

A tear rolled down my nose to my whiskers. "Are you sure you will be okay? What about Aunt Sibel?" I asked.

"Don't worry." Mina showed me the keys. The metal shone in the moonlight. "It will all be fine. You've helped me set things right. If it weren't for you, I never could've done it."

I stared at her for a moment. *Set things right.* That's what Zehra Hala had said I needed to do, but I couldn't see how she would've known about my adventures as a cat and how it would turn out. The words were probably a coincidence – that's all they were.

Mina embraced me one last time, then I gazed at the twinkling skyline of Istanbul over the Bosphorus, the perfect moon sliding over the water as sailing boats broke the waves, the speared minaret towers of the Hagia Sophia pointing upwards to the stars over the city wall's sentinel gates. The men had started to call from their balconies, their prayerful song rising as the white cranes mounted the sky to do their dance.

Mina's father called to her.

"I should go. You should too," said Mina. "It's time."

I nodded and unrolled the parchment paper. The ink shimmered in the silvery moonlight and the image of my face moved, smiling and laughing. I waved goodbye one last time, then reached out my paw to touch the image, and the world went dark around me.

17

HOME

The sun lit a yellow square around me on a wooden floor. I glanced down at my body. My whiskers were gone, my fur was gone, my paws were gone and my tail was gone. I stretched my arms and legs, checking every inch. Mustafa had done it – I was myself again!

I got to my feet and looked around the room. It wasn't much larger than a walk-in wardrobe. A red tulip painting hung on the wall and a frilly yellow blanket decorated the twin bed that was by the window. This was my room – the one I'd stayed in the first night at Zehra Hala's house.

"Baba?" I called out.

I dashed down the hallway to the entrance hall. The chandelier twinkled in the morning sun and the plush silk rug glowed red.

It didn't make sense. When I'd followed the cat upstairs and found the bottle, the windows had been broken, the curtains shredded, the walls buckling and the floors rotted. The house still looked old, but it wasn't run-down anymore. Someone had taken care of the place. The floors were varnished, the walls were painted and the curtains were clean.

My chest tightened in panic. Something was off – Mustafa had tricked me again.

I raced up the stairs to Mina's room. Just as I remembered, there was a window next to a door that led to a small balcony, enclosed on all sides by wooden screens with cutout holes the shape of four-leafed clovers. But my purple suitcase was next to the bed. Everything was different, yet it was all the same.

I fell to my knees. Before Mina and I had left for the Grand Bazaar, she'd tucked the riddle back under the loose floorboard. I pulled back the Turkish rug and ran my hand over the wooden floor, checking for irregularities. I found it – the loose board was still there. I pried it up and stuck my hand into the hole, but there was nothing.

"I know what you are searching for," said Zehra Hala, standing in the doorway. She leaned heavily on her cane. "You won't find it."

She shuffled inside and squeaked down on the bed. "When I was young, my mother, Mina, told me a fascinating story about a cat who changed her life. She said, 'If it hadn't been for that cat, I never would have found the courage to stand up to Aunt Sibel and send a letter asking my father to come home. Aunt Sibel would've spent the family fortune and left us in poverty.'" Zehra Hala watched me carefully. "I did not believe her story until this moment, when you looked under the floorboard."

"But . . . how do you know what I'm looking for?" I asked.

"My mother told me someone would come looking for this one day." Zehra Hala's hand shook as she pulled a yellowed piece of paper from her pocket and handed it to me. It was the drawing of my face, the one I'd used to get back home, only now the paper was tattered, and the silvery magic ink had faded to pale grey.

"The child looks remarkably similar to you, don't you think?" asked Zehra Hala.

I was quiet, not knowing what to say. No one would believe me if I told them my incredible story.

Zehra Hala slanted her eyes at me, then shrugged. "We are all entitled to a few secrets," she said. "This house has seen powerful magic. I can sense it. Magic leaves a trace. It clings to the shadows and hides in the dark, but you can feel it watching you. Sometimes, as I'm about to fall asleep, I can see it, like a double vision. This other house is dusty and cold, full of sadness, run-down. It's a vision of my life as a different story. An unhappy one. It's a peculiar vision, and it's always the same. But then I blink, and it's gone," she said. "Maybe this doesn't make sense to you."

I rocked back onto my heels. It did make sense to me, actually, but I couldn't tell her that without explaining why. "What happened to Mina?"

"How do you mean?" asked Zehra Hala.

"Her father came home, and she told him about Aunt Sibel. What happened after that?" I asked.

"It was quite the scandal. Mina's father was a travelling merchant. He sent all sorts of presents to her. Pretty dresses, toys, shoes. The finest of everything. Aunt Sibel, who was supposed to be looking after Mina, stole everything her father had sent to Mina and sold it to the highest bidder, and then kept the gold for herself. When Mina's father came home, they opened Aunt Sibel's cupboard and found the gold she'd been hiding. She confessed that she'd planned to run away with the money and live like a princess on the Mediterranean coast. She would've left Mina and her father with almost nothing."

"What happened to Aunt Sibel?" I asked.

"Mina's father sent her away with only the clothes on her back. He told her that she was never to set foot in his house again. They heard some years later that she ended up washing dishes in a teahouse. Mina always found this amusing, as she said Aunt Sibel didn't care for washing dishes."

A proud grin grew on my face. Mina had *done* it – she'd stood up to Aunt Sibel and got rid of her.

Zehra Hala glanced out the window like she was lost in memory. "My mother was an interesting person. When she had her portrait painted, she insisted the artist draw a cat on her lap."

The painting I'd seen in the hallway when I'd first arrived . . . Wow. . . . The cat in the picture was *me*. I let out a laugh. "She does sound like an interesting person."

"I miss her," said Zehra Hala.

I nodded sympathetically.

I missed her too, but I would never forget her.

Zehra Hala folded my hand in hers and patted it warmly.

There was still one thing I didn't understand. The house looked *different* now. "But the mansion is so . . . nice," I murmured to myself without thinking. "Why would anyone sell it?"

Zehra Hala raised her eyebrows in surprise. "Sell it? This old place is like a member of our family. We would never sell it! We just had it refurbished a few years ago."

I blinked at her, trying to understand how everything had changed. Baba and I weren't here to sell the house?

Zehra Hala patted my arm. "I am very glad you and your Baba finally got a chance to come and visit. I've been asking him to bring you here over the summer holidays for a long time."

My mind hummed as the pieces came together like a puzzle. Aunt Sibel was the reason our family had lost its fortune. The family hadn't been able to care for the mansion, so it had fallen into disrepair. When Mina had got rid of Aunt Sibel, she'd changed everything – she'd *set things right* – and I had helped her. We'd both turned out to be the family secret, like Mustafa's riddle said we would be.

Baba's footsteps thumped down the hallway and barged through the door. "Dalya?" he said.

I threw my arms around him as he kneeled down for a hug. He was warm and smelled of his aftershave, like I remembered, but his arms were shaking.

"Didn't you hear me calling for you?" His eyes were rimmed with red. "I had the worst nightmare last night," he said. "You were gone, and I found myself standing at the top of the stairs, screaming – "

"I'm home. I'm right here." I leaned my forehead against his. "I'm not going anywhere." Tears streaked down my cheeks in two straight lines.

His phone buzzed in his pocket. As he took it out, disappointment sank to my stomach.

"You have to work?" I asked.

After I was turned into a cat, all I'd wanted was to get back to him. I'd hoped everything would be different.

But it didn't matter how much I had changed, if he wasn't willing to change too.

The phone buzzed in his pocket again.

He took it out and pressed the button to ignore the call, then he pulled off his headset and switched off his phone. "No, I'm not going to work."

I looked at him, surprised.

"I brought you here so we could be together. I promised we'd spend time together while were here, and I broke that promise yesterday. I'm sorry, Dalya. I know I need to change. You're the most important thing in my life, more important than anything else, and I want you to know that. I'm going to do better. For you, for both of us." He held my face in his hands. "Give me another chance?"

Somehow he'd found all the words I'd needed to hear and said them all at once. It felt like a door inside me had been thrown open and all my emotions had spilled out. I couldn't tell if I wanted to laugh or cry. My cheeks burned pink as I wrapped my arms around his neck. "Yes, Baba. I want that."

We held each other for a moment, then he took my chin in his hand and let his eyes wander over my face. "That dream was so real," he said.

I wanted to tell him it *was* real – it wasn't a dream. That I'd really been gone, and I'd been scared. More than anything, I was glad to be back.

I patted my throat to check if my necklace was still there, then I rolled the blue eye pendant between my fingers. The green ribbon Mina had tied on the pendant was still there. I rubbed my finger over the fabric. The necklace was special to me because Zehra Hala had given it to me, and now it was doubly special because I still had Mina's ribbon. I stood there for a moment, seesawing between belief and disbelief, until my mind finally held steady for a moment, balancing on a single thought: *I'd made it home safely.*

We stood next to the window. The courtyard was no longer a wild jumble of leaves. Neat rows of bushes and lemon trees ringed the fence, allowing a spectacular view to the bottom of the hill, where the blue waves of the Bosphorus sparkled and the seagulls spun in the salt air. The view I'd seen from the city walls with Salyangoz hadn't had high-rises or cars, but some things had stayed the same: On the other side of the bay, I spotted the spiky minaret towers of the Hagia Sophia, the round domes of the Grand Bazaar and the tall gates of Topkapi Palace.

Between bushy trees, sections of the old city wall appeared.

"I was thinking we could go sightseeing today. I grew up around this neighbourhood, and I'd like to show it to you," Baba said.

I nodded eagerly, then smiled at him. "Do you remember singing to me when I was little?"

He raised his eyebrows in surprise. "What made you think of that?"

I shrugged. "Maybe you could teach me some of the songs. I'd like to learn."

His hazel eyes shone. "I'd love that. You are such a wonderful child, Dalya." He kissed my cheek. "Mashallah."

When I'd first heard that word, it hadn't meant anything to me. I understood it now, at least a little. Baba was asking to keep me safe and protected because he loved me, and he was saying it with his whole heart.

"I love you so much, Baba." I wrapped my arms around his neck again.

Salyangoz was right: Mashallah was bigger than one word. It was a whole rainbow of feelings, and I felt every colour sparkle inside me.

A gust of late summer wind kicked up. Pink streaked the dawn sky. The tidy courtyard smelled sweet, like honeysuckle. I stood next to Baba, purple suitcase in hand, ready to go to the airport. It was time for school again.

He'd kept his promise, taking me to all the best sights in

the old city and telling me about the city's history. He showed me the park where he played football as a boy and the shop where he'd spent his pocket money buying pistachio ice cream. I told him about the Rat Bazaar, the gold-crowned pigeon, the whirling cranes and the court of the Cat Sultan. He laughed and said I had a wild imagination, but I knew better. Someday I'd find those places again, even if it was only in my dreams.

As we turned to leave, I took a final look at the house. Everything had changed. There was no paint peeling from the exterior, no buckling roof, no cracked windows, no slanted front door. I'd been so scared when I'd first arrived, hating the idea of living there, but now I didn't want to leave. This was *my family's house* – a place I could belong – that summer, and every summer after.

Zehra Hala was right: Any place can be home if you keep an open heart. It was the truest thing I'd ever heard – I knew it, because I'd found it in Istanbul.

ACKNOWLEDGEMENTS

This book started as a bedtime story for my daughter, who wanted to hear a tale about the street cat we'd just met at the Hagia Sophia. *Dalya and the Magic Ink Bottle* is far from that first iteration, but at its heart, it's still a love letter to Istanbul and its famous feline residents, and I hope readers enjoy it as much as my children did.

The book went through a number of transformations before it took this final form, and I owe many thanks:

To my agent, Moe Ferrara, who believed in this book and stood by me through the whole process. I am grateful for your wise guidance.

To my editor, Michelle Bisson, for making me cut things that didn't work and improve things that did. You pushed me to do better.

To my early readers, Jason Latshaw, Paul Taegel, Barbara Curry, and especially Austin Formato. I wouldn't have got here without your unflagging support through the twists and turns of this writerly journey.

To Kat Howard, S.A. Chakraborty, and everyone who commented on this manuscript at various stages, and to my mentor, Fonda Lee, who gave me a sage piece of advice when I needed it most.

To my dear friends Jessica Yingling, Jenna Milly and Susan Hurwitz Arneson, who never let me lose hope.

To my sister-in-law Simla Olgun, who provided invaluable information about Istanbul's history.

To my mother, for years of listening kindly and patiently, and my father, for making me laugh.

Last, but never least, to my husband, for giving me time and space to write, and to my children, for letting me tell them stories. My love for you is richer than my tongue.

ABOUT THE AUTHOR

J.M. Evenson holds a PhD from the
University of Michigan, USA, and a
master's of fine arts from UCLA.
As a screenwriter in Los Angeles,
she worked as a consultant at Netflix;
pitched and developed ideas at
production houses from DreamWorks
to Focus Features; and taught writing
at Pepperdine University. She visits
Istanbul yearly to see family and lives
in Los Angeles with her husband
and kids.